HAUNTED ISLAND

**Look for these and
other APPLE PAPERBACKS
in your local bookstore!**

HAUNTED ISLAND

Joan Lowery Nixon

AN
APPLE
PAPERBACK

SCHOLASTIC INC.
New York Toronto London Auckland Sydney

ISBN 0-590-43134-X

12   7 8 9/9 0/0

Printed in the U.S.A.   40

1

Chris Holt leaned on the railing of the wide porch that stretched across the length of his Aunt Jennie's Island View Inn. He stared at the carpenter who stood below him, talking to Aunt Jennie.

The man tugged at a strap on his bib overalls and twisted his shoulders as though he'd like to squirm out of what he had to say. "Nobody's going to work on your island, ma'am. Not a man in these parts is willing to set foot on the place."

Amy, Chris's twelve-year-old sister, tiptoed to the rail and nudged his arm. "You shouldn't be listening to someone else's conversation," she whispered.

"Go away," Chris whispered back, missing whatever Aunt Jennie had said to the carpenter.

"Just because you're a year older than me — " Amy began, but Chris interrupted her.

"They're talking about the island," he said.

"Oh." She automatically looked up and across

1

the wide stretch of the Mississippi River to the small, wooded island near the middle of the river.

The carpenter was speaking again. "You may think you own that island, Miz Parker," he said.

"But I do own it!" Aunt Jennie's voice became higher-pitched. "The island came with this property the Island View Inn is on. I have the papers to prove it!"

The carpenter shook his head. "What I'm trying to say, ma'am, is that you may own the paper on the island, but it don't really belong to you. It belongs to the ghosts of Joshua Hanover and that monstrous black dog of his — the one called 'Shadow.' "

"That's — that's ridiculous!" Aunt Jennie sputtered. "How can you possibly believe in ghosts?"

"Because they're there," he answered. "Now, you want me to fix that broken gutter on the north side?"

"I — I suppose so. Yes," Aunt Jennie answered.

The carpenter looked up at Chris and Amy and gave them a quick twist of a smile. "Your kids look a lot like you with that black hair," he said. "Tall like you, too. Sure handsome children you got there, ma'am."

"My children?" She glanced at Chris and Amy with surprise, and Chris realized she hadn't known they were on the porch. "Oh, you mean Amy and

Chris. They're my niece and nephew. They're visiting here with my sister, Elizabeth Holt. They're all helping me put this inn together."

She introduced them, and the carpenter nodded. "Good luck to you, ma'am," he said, and headed for the north side of the inn.

"Good luck, my foot!" Aunt Jennie grumbled, as she plopped down on the bottom step of the stairs to the porch, her elbows propped on her knees, her chin resting in her hands.

Chris and Amy raced each other to join her on the steps.

"I can't believe this is happening," Aunt Jennie said. "I loved this old house the first time I saw it, and I knew that with some imagination and hard work I could make it into a beautiful inn. But it had to have something special going for it to attract visitors who would want to stay a few days." She shook her head. "When I found that the property included that lovely little island with the sheltered beach, I knew that was the answer, so I bought the property."

Chris looked across at the island. It was too far away to make out many details, but he could see the strip of beach and the thick cluster of pines that covered the island. With the sun on the island he was able to make out a shape that looked like part of a roof with a chimney.

"There's a house on the island," he said.

3

But Aunt Jennie hadn't heard him. He wasn't sure if she was talking to herself or to them. "I planned to have rowboats and sailboats and picnic excursions for guests at the inn, and summer beach parties — all sorts of fun that the big hotels near the city can't offer. Since this part of Missouri is limestone country, there should even be small caves on the island to explore. But if no one will work on the island, my plans will fail."

She gave a long sigh and added, "The island fun was my one chance to attract guests away from the large hotels. If I can't get enough guests, I could possibly lose the inn. All because the people who live here believe some silly stories about the island being haunted and even call it "Haunted Island!"

"Tell us the stories," Chris said.

"I can't remember them," Aunt Jennie said. "I was so busy making lists of repairs and supplies and all the things I had to do, that I really didn't pay attention."

"If somebody told me there was a ghost on my property, I'd want to know all about it," Amy said.

"Sure you would," Chris said. "And then you'd run screaming to Mom."

"I would not."

"Okay," Chris said, and leaned across Aunt Jennie toward Amy, curling his hands like claws and making his voice as deep as he could. "It's a

monster ghost with eyes that glow in the dark
and — ”

"Stop it!" Amy slapped her hands over her ears.

"As a matter of fact, there did happen to be
something about eyes that glow," Aunt Jennie
said. "Wait! I know! The ghost is supposed to have
fiery eyes."

"And his name is Joshua Hanover," Chris said.

"How would you know?" Amy asked.

"That's the name the carpenter said. And he
also told us the ghost had a big black dog named
Shadow."

Amy shivered. "I'd hate to meet a dog ghost!"

"Don't worry. If he's a ghost, you won't meet
him. There aren't any such things as ghosts,"
Aunt Jennie said. She stood up and stretched.
"Back to work. Your mom and I are determined
to finish wallpapering the bathrooms before dinner." She sighed. "We've had so much rain it's
delayed all the repair work, and there's still
so much to do."

"Let us help," Chris said.

"Not with the wallpapering," Aunt Jennie said.
"That's too tricky. How would you like to put a
coat of white paint on the porch railings? I don't
think it will rain again for another couple of days.
The paint should dry."

"Sure," Chris said. "We can do that."

"You'll be very careful?"

"We're always very careful, Aunt Jennie." Chris and Amy jumped up at the same time, bouncing off each other and flopping down to the steps again.

"Well, most of the time we are," Amy said, rubbing her shoulder and laughing.

"We promise to do a good job," Chris said.

"Thanks," Aunt Jennie said. "And maybe tomorrow you could tackle these old wicker rockers. If they're painted white, too, they'll look lovely lined up on the porch where visitors can sit and admire the view."

Chris and Amy helped Aunt Jennie get the paint, brushes, rags, and turpentine, and they set to work.

The porch was long, and the top rail had many supports, each of them carved round and round with intricate loops and whorls and tiny cutouts — all of which had to be carefully painted, making the job of painting last much longer than Chris and Amy had expected.

The river glowed red and gold, mirroring the setting sun, by the time Chris stood and admired the gleaming railing. "That's that," he said. "We did it."

"And without getting paint on the floor boards of the porch," Amy said smugly.

The screen door behind them slapped back into place as their mother came out of the house. "The railing looks wonderful!" she said. "You're wonderful. Our wallpapering job is wonderful." She took a deep breath of the pines and added, "This whole place is wonderful, isn't it? I hope with all my heart that it's successful for Jennie."

"Did she tell you about the ghosts?" Amy asked.

"Ghosts? Baloney!" their mom said. She laughed, and her laugh was a lot like her sister's laugh, Chris thought. Even their brown eyes sparkled in the same way. It would be easy for anyone to tell they were sisters.

"And speaking of baloney," their mother said, "Jennie and I are getting hungry. Want some dinner?"

"Sure," Amy said. "Want me to set the table?"

"Thanks, but not tonight," their mother said. "We're too tired. Jennie is putting some sandwich makings and potato chips and tomato slices on the dining room table, so dinner will be a do-it-yourself meal, and you can have it whenever you want."

They cleaned their brushes and their hands as fast as they could and hurried into the house. After scrubbing off the turpentine and making gigantic sandwiches with everything inside them except the potato chips, Amy said, "Let's take these out to the porch."

"You'll smell the paint," Chris warned.

"It's not that bad. Besides, Mom and Aunt Jennie are talking about room rates and plumbing bills and stuff that isn't very interesting. If we sit outside in the dark we can watch the fireflies."

"Okay," Chris said, and followed his sister outside and down the porch stairs to the bottom step. The moon was so large that it touched the trees and grass with a yellow glow and silvered the surface of the river. Even the dark little island was frosted by the moonlight, and scatters of fireflies blinked and winked around them.

For a while they were busy making their sandwiches disappear, but finally Amy put her empty paper plate on the step next to her and said, "When you were reading all those history books about this area, did you read anything about Aunt Jennie's island?"

"I don't know," Chris said.

"How could you not know?"

"Because the island doesn't have a name."

"It must have had some kind of a name. Someone was living on it."

"I wish I could have been one of the pioneers who settled this territory," Chris said. "Just imagine how exciting it would have been to explore this country."

Amy groaned. "Don't start telling me again about all that pioneer stuff. Ever since you did that school project on pioneer life and took that wilderness trip, you've driven me crazy talking about it. Besides, I want to talk about Aunt Jennie's island."

"What about the island?"

8

"Chris, do you think that the island is really haunted?"

"No," Chris said. "Aunt Jennie and Mom are right. There aren't any such things as ghosts."

"Then why won't anyone around here go to the island?"

"I don't know," Chris said. "But I wish we knew the real story about the island, because maybe we could prove to everybody that it's not haunted."

"Then Aunt Jennie could have the boats and picnics and all that stuff she wants." Amy sighed. "But how will we find out?"

Behind them in the dark shadows a soft voice spoke. "I could tell you. I was there."

2

Chris jumped up so fast the paper plate flew from his lap, and Amy gave a little shriek.

"Who's there?" Chris demanded.

The voice spoke again. "I'm Amos Corley. Come up here and join me."

As Chris and Amy climbed the stairs they stared into the deep shadows where the moonlight couldn't reach. There sat an elderly man rocking gently back and forth in one of the old wicker rocking chairs.

"I'm sorry I screamed," Amy said. "I didn't hear you come out on the porch."

Amos Corley was short, stocky, and almost completely bald, with only a few wisps of gray hair curling over his ears. He wore faded overalls, too, so Chris decided he must be one of the many workmen and repairmen who had been hired by Aunt Jennie to help put the inn in shape. But he didn't remember seeing Mr. Corley around the inn. "Have you been working here?" Chris asked.

"I've been here many times," Amos told him. "I come around when I'm wanted."

Chris remembered his manners and stopped staring. "This is my sister, Amy Holt," Chris said. "And — "

"And you're Chris Holt," Amos added. "Pleased to meet you both."

Chris was startled that the man knew his name, but Amy didn't seem to notice. She blurted out, "Mr. Corley, you said you could tell us the story about the island. Will you? Will you tell us right now?"

"That's what your brother wished for," Amos said. He leaned toward Chris. "Are you really sure that you want to hear it?"

"Of course we are!" Amy said, before Chris had a chance to answer.

She tugged one of the rockers close to Amos's rocker, and Chris sat cross-legged on the floor, facing the old man.

Chris nodded, uncomfortable because Amos was still staring at him. "Yes," he said, and immediately had the strange feeling that he should have answered no. But before Chris could change his mind Amos Corley had begun the story.

"When I was a boy — about the same age as you, Chris — I worked for Joshua Hanover," Amos said. "And I was there on that horrible day when the earth quaked so violently that the river changed

11

its course, creating the island, and Joshua screamed that he would never rest until he was avenged." Amos paused, then continued the story:

Joshua Hanover was tall and thin. His arms dangled as though they were too long for his body, and his hair stuck out from under his hat like wisps of pale straw. Behind his back, some people laughed and called him a scarecrow.

He was mean enough to scare away anyone, not just crows. With his mouth turned down and a perpetual scowl on his face, he barely spoke to the townspeople when he had to go into town for supplies. A few times he had shouted at some children who were walking on the road past his farm, warning them not to trespass. None of them would have wanted to, even before his warnings. Everyone was glad enough to keep a safe distance from Joshua Hanover.

He was called a miser and a penny pincher by anyone who had business dealings with him. Joshua had been one of the first settlers in this part of the territory, claiming much of the valuable land near the river. As the town developed and grew, the river land was needed. He sold some of it, setting a fair price, as he said, and refusing to bargain. He was as suspicious of banks as he was of his neighbors, so he refused to set foot in the bank. It was rumored that Joshua kept his money in a large canvas sack that was guarded well by his dog, Shadow.

Joshua and Shadow were well suited to each other. Shadow was a large black dog with gleaming eyes and sharp teeth, and just as mean as his master.

But Joshua and Shadow weren't the only ones who lived on the Hanover farm. I came to live there, too. When my parents died I left our farm and walked north into Missouri territory, a boy of thirteen, without family or home. I worked at odd jobs along the way, and I'd stay in a place as long as I was needed and fed and had a warm place to sleep.

Since I was unfamiliar with this place I hadn't heard about Joshua Hanover. I saw the farmhouse from the road, and it looked like a comfortable, tidy place. It faced the road, but was close by the river.

"On the island," Amy interrupted.

"There was no island yet," Amos said. "I'll get to that later."

"Don't interrupt," Chris said to Amy.

Amos continued.

Near the house I could see a short wooden pier and an open rowboat tied to a piling. Beyond the house and barn the wide pasture swept up the

13

hill. The sides and crest of the hill were covered with a thick piney woods. There was no smoke coming from the chimney of the house and no smell of dinner cooking, even though it was close to noon. Maybe the people here could use an extra hand, I thought, so I walked up the narrow road that led to the house.

I had one hand raised in the air, ready to knock at the front door, when I heard a deep growl behind me. I turned quickly to see a terrifying black dog with his mouth pulled open to show sharp fangs. The dog stood motionless, poised to spring.

"Help!" I tried to call, but the word came out a whisper. The dog seemed to move closer, and this time I was so scared that I hollered loudly, "Help!"

"Stay, Shadow!" The voice was sharp and unfriendly, but I was glad to see a tall man come around the corner of the house. The man stopped next to the dog, and I was surprised to see that the man and the dog had the same angry glint in their eyes.

"What do you think you're doing here?" the man growled at me.

"I'm sorry, sir," I said. "I didn't mean any harm. I'm traveling through, and I'm looking for work and a place to stay."

"What kind of work do you do?"

"Anything," I told him. "I can do any kind of

outdoor work, and I even do chores inside the house, if the lady of the house needs a helping hand."

"Hmmm," the man said. He looked hard at me. "So you can clean. Can you cook, too?"

"Pretty good." Matter of fact, I was stretching the truth. When Ma was sick I had learned how to make boiled beef brisket that wasn't too tough, and beaten biscuits that weren't too flat; and I could slice a slab of bacon thin enough so that it would fry up crisp — if I watched it closely and was careful not to burn it. My cooking was nothing to brag on, but you wouldn't die if you ate it.

The man waited a few minutes, then suddenly said, "I'm Joshua Hanover. I could use some help in the house, so you can sleep in the barn and stay as long as I think you're worth your keep."

"Thank you, sir. I'll be a big help to your wife," I answered.

"Haven't got a wife," Joshua snapped. "Now go inside and see what you can do about getting something on the table for the noon meal."

The dog hadn't moved. His teeth were still bared. I didn't move, either. "What about the dog, sir? I don't think he likes me."

"Shadow? 'Course he doesn't like you," Joshua said. "Shadow doesn't like anybody, but he'll leave you alone if you leave him alone." He muttered a few words to the dog, who relaxed and slowly sat.

He looked more like a normal dog now, but he still kept his sharp eyes on me.

It didn't take long to find out that there was a lot more work to be done than I'd thought. The outside of the house and the land around it were well kept, but the inside of the house needed to be swept and scrubbed and painted. I worked hard, and soon the rooms were a lot cleaner. Joshua didn't have much laid by in the way of food, but the second day I was in that house I went down in the cellar to see what I could find. Just as I had thought, there was a bin, and in the bin were stored some carrots and potatoes. I took some upstairs with me and fixed them for dinner. I wasn't too good at cooking vegetables, so they were kind of mushy from being overcooked, but at least they made more of a meal than just meat and bread.

I was real proud of the platter of boiled beef and the large bowl of potato and carrot chunks I put in front of Joshua Hanover. But when he came to the kitchen table and saw the meal, he suddenly gripped the edge of the table and shouted, "Where did you get those vegetables?"

"In the cellar, Mr. Hanover," I said, wondering what was the matter. They didn't look that bad.

Joshua was so angry that it frightened me. "You're never to go down in the cellar! Never again! Do you understand me?" he yelled.

"But since that's where you keep the vegetables — "

Joshua interrupted me. "You tell me when you need carrots and potatoes, and I'll bring them up to you. Have you got that straight?"

"Yes, sir," I whispered.

We ate the meal in silence, while I wondered what Joshua kept in the cellar. Obviously, it was something he didn't want me to see. I was curious, but not curious enough to want to find out — not when every time I thought about sneaking down into the cellar to take a look around I could remember the furious gleam in Joshua Hanover's eyes.

I was well worth my keep. I kept to the chores, only once in a great while taking a few minutes to walk along the riverbank and peer into the small limestone caves that dotted the hill. There were times when I wished for a friend to explore with, but I had been born to a life of work, not play, and I accepted it.

Joshua never complimented me for the work I did, except for one day when he looked around the room as though it was the first time he'd seen it and said, "I like having the house tidied up."

"Thank you, sir," I said.

But Joshua scowled again and added, "Things could be better, though. Can't say much that's good about your cooking."

I had been at the Hanover farm for about three months when one Tuesday morning Joshua set up the tub, heated buckets of water on the wood stove, and sent me out to do chores in the barn.

I stared at the tub. "You're going to take a bath?" I asked. "But it's Tuesday, Mr. Hanover, not Saturday."

"Never you mind," Joshua said. "I've got a reason."

After a while he called me to come back to the house. By this time Joshua was shaved and dressed in clean clothes. "We're going to town," he told me. "You and Shadow can ride in the back of the wagon."

I didn't like being that close to Shadow, but I didn't have a choice. I hugged my side of the wagon, hanging on tightly as it bounced in and over the ruts in the road. I was relieved that Shadow sat staring out the other side of the wagon, ignoring me.

We drove past the block of stores in the small town, and some of the people on the street stared to see Joshua Hanover dressed up and riding into town. A few people followed the wagon, and I knew they were as curious as I was about what Joshua was up to.

Joshua tied the horse's reins to the rack in front of Owens's dry goods store, then stepped up onto the wooden sidewalk. I was unsure of what was going to happen, so I stayed where I was, even though the heat of the midday sun made sweat run down my back.

"Do you want me to carry anything from the store?" I asked him.

"Don't need anything," he said. He pulled out a large, round pocket watch and looked at it. "I'm waiting for the stage to get here."

In a short while we could hear the sound of horses' hooves and the rattle of the stagecoach as it approached the town. By this time others had come to wait, too, many of them curious people who liked to watch the stagecoach arrive and depart, since it didn't come more than a couple of times a month. Today Joshua seemed to be more interesting to the people than the stagecoach, so there was a little group standing at one side, watching him as the coach bounced and clattered around the bend in the road, and the driver pulled his sweaty horses to a stop.

Joshua moved forward and waited. As the dust settled around the coach wheels, the driver jumped from his platform and opened the stagecoach door. Everyone watched eagerly to see who would step down from the coach.

3

"Who was it?" Amy asked.

"Give Mr. Corley a chance," Chris said, "and he'll tell us."

Mr. Corley nodded and continued his story.

A young woman stepped off the stagecoach, carrying a small satchel and taking the driver's hand to keep her balance. She wasn't pretty. Her clothes were plain and looked too big for her, and her brown hair was pulled tightly into a knot at the back of her neck. Her only jewelry was a thin, twisted gold chain that she wore around her neck. Her eyes were wide and a little bit scared as she peered out from under the brim of a black straw hat.

Joshua took a step forward. His perpetual scowl seemed even deeper. "Are you Amelia Jones?" he asked.

Her chin quivered, as though she was going to

cry, but she raised her chin, took a deep breath, and said, "Yes. I'm Amelia Jones. I'm here to marry Joshua Hanover."

Some of the folks in the crowd murmured and gasped at that, but Joshua paid no mind to them and spoke up.

"I'm Joshua Hanover," he said. "My wagon's over there. Just follow me."

He started to turn, but Amelia held out her satchel to him. He blinked at it for a minute, as though he was wondering what to do with it, then took it from her and carried it to the wagon. Amelia followed.

Shadow growled low in his throat, but Joshua told him to be quiet. "That's my dog, Shadow," he said. "He won't bother you after he gets used to you." He climbed up on the seat and said to Amelia, "Hurry up. Let's get going."

But before she climbed up on the high seat with Joshua, she looked at me, and for the first time she smiled. "Who's this?" she said. "You didn't say you had a son."

"He's not my son," Joshua said. "He's just a boy who works around the place." He picked up the reins and clucked at the horse.

"But he has a name," Amelia said. She smiled at me again. "What's your name, young man?"

"Amos Corley," I answered, smiling back.

"Let's go," Joshua snapped. Amelia climbed on the seat and held on tightly as the wagon jerked into motion.

The horse began plodding down the main street of town. Joshua didn't say anything, so Amelia twisted to look at me. "Do you live here in town?" she asked.

"No, ma'am," I said. "I'm just working my way north. I'm an orphan."

"So am I," Amelia said, and smiled.

I wondered why I had thought she was plain. Her smile made her whole face light up. I liked her smile, and I liked Amelia.

Joshua pulled up the horse so abruptly that Amelia lost her balance and almost fell from the wagon. "Here's where we meet the county judge who'll marry us," Joshua said. He waited a minute while Amelia smoothed down her skirt and adjusted her hat. "You want to change your mind?"

She took a long look at him. "No," she said. "Might as well go forward. I've got nothing to go back to."

Joshua tied the horse to the nearest post and turned to me just as I was climbing out of the wagon. "You stay here with Shadow. This won't take long."

Amelia looked so scared I thought she needed a friend with her, and I wanted to be her friend.

"I've never been to a wedding," I complained. "I'd like to come, too."

Before Joshua could answer, Amelia spoke up. "Weddings have got to have witnesses," she said. "Amos can be our witness."

Joshua didn't say a word. He walked up the wooden steps and into the office of the county judge. I hopped down from the wagon, and Amelia and I followed him.

He was right. The ceremony took just a couple of minutes. The judge read it from a book. Joshua and Amelia said, "I will," or something like that, and the judge told them they were married. They both signed their names on a paper, and we left to go directly to the farm.

It was nice having Amelia there. She thought of all sorts of things to do to that house besides cleaning it. She painted the inside walls white and made some blue-and-white flowered curtains and planted some flowers by the front door. Sometimes she rowed out in the little boat and fished and brought back a good supply of catfish for dinner, which she fried up with cornmeal all brown and crunchy on the outside and flaky and delicious on the inside.

Could she cook! She made a mutton stew good enough to brag on, and biscuits that rose high and light, and a squash pie with cinnamon and nutmeg that smelled almost as good as it tasted.

Some ladies from the town came to call on Amelia, but Joshua let it be known that he didn't welcome visitors, so the ladies stopped coming. If Amelia was lonely or unhappy, she didn't let on. She was shy, she was plain, but she was practical. She was determined to be a good wife, and she was.

I liked to talk to Amelia, so I stuck around. That seemed to be all right with Joshua. He just set me to jobs out in the barn and the fields. I'd hurry to get to meals before Joshua would, just so I'd have a few minutes to listen to Amelia and what she had to say. She told me that she had no living relatives and had answered Joshua's ad for a wife, which he'd put in a Boston newspaper. The gold chain, which she wore every day, was her only tie to the parents she had lost when she was young, and it was the only possession she treasured.

Amelia had very few possessions, and I don't think Joshua gave her anything besides a thin, plain wedding ring. He was a strange person. It was easy to see that he liked Amelia. I think he actually fell in love with her. But love didn't make him happier. It seemed to make him meaner.

He acted suspicious of anyone who spoke to her when they went to town for supplies, and was jealous of anyone she talked to. As the cold weather came on, Amelia insisted that I be allowed to spend some time after dinner in the house, where it was light and warm, instead of in the small room I'd made for myself in the barn. Joshua finally agreed, but he hardly had a word to say to me, and I honestly thought he'd soon be sending me on my way.

Shadow didn't like Amelia, even though she gave him some choice scraps and always made sure his water bowl was filled with fresh water. I think he was jealous of her being there. He'd curl up near the fire and close his eyelids, looking as though he had gone to sleep. His breathing would be steady and heavy, whistling through his nose. But he wasn't really asleep. If anyone had looked closely, they'd have seen tiny, gleaming slits, where he was peeking through. All evening Shadow would keep his eyes on Amelia, watching her every move. I think she was a little scared of him. I know he scared me.

One frosty morning — December 12, I well remember — I went to the house with my arms full of firewood. Amelia let me in and helped me pile the wood in the bin near the big iron stove. She'd put a big bowl of red apples on the table and arranged some short pine boughs around it.

Besides the big apron she wore over her clothes during the day, she had a cloth tied over her head.

"I'm going to tackle some heavy cleaning," she told me. She cocked her head to one side and looked at me. "Want to help?"

"Yes, ma'am," I said. "What do you want me to do?"

"Help me move some of that rubbish in the cellar."

I gasped. "But Mr. Hanover won't let me go into the cellar."

Amelia shrugged. "Well, he hasn't done a thing to clean it up, and I don't like living over such a dump heap. End of an old year, start of a new, the house should be clean from top to bottom."

"One day I went down just to get some carrots and potatoes from the bin," I said, "and he got real mad. He told me never to go down there again. Didn't he tell you that, too?"

"There's no telling what gets that man upset," she said, and for a moment she got a sad, faraway look, as though she was thinking about something else. Then she shook her head a little and picked up the broom. "Whatever reason he's got for not wanting anyone down in the cellar isn't enough," she said. "Even though it is just a dirt floor cellar, it's thick with dust and needs cleaning out. Besides, I'm his wife. I ought to be able to clean the cellar if I want to."

I didn't want Joshua Hanover to be angry with me, but I didn't want Amelia Hanover to have to tackle that job by herself. My friendship for Amelia was stronger than my fear of Joshua. I would do anything for her, so I said, "Just tell me what you want me to do."

"Bring a lantern," she said. "We'll clean out every crack and corner."

I lit a lantern and followed her down the cellar stairs.

There were boxes and barrels, and piles of old rusted tools, and a few broken bottles and jars, and some moth-eaten rags, and dirt everywhere.

"Move that big box in the corner," Amelia said.

I did, and a rat ran out, right over my feet.

Amelia didn't shriek. She just swatted at him with the broom, but he ducked into a hole in the wall and disappeared. "After we clean this place, let's board up that hole," she said.

We used an empty box to carry up loads of rubbish and dirt, and after a while the cellar began to look a lot better.

"Over there — under the stairs," Amelia told me. "Something is crammed under there. Can you pull it out?"

I got down on my knees and tugged. It was a canvas sack of some sort and fairly heavy. I dragged it out where we could see it. The top was folded over and lashed with a buckle.

"What in the world is that?" Amelia asked. "Can you open it?"

I opened the leather thong and the buckle and spread the top of the sack wide. The lantern gleamed on the contents. Inside the sack, almost to the brim, were silver coins.

"Oh, dear!" Amelia gasped and took a step backward.

"So that's why — " I began, but a terrible sound choked off whatever I was going to say.

Behind us, on the stairs, was a loud, growling noise. We whirled around to face the sound, and I honestly couldn't say if the growl came from Shadow or Joshua Hanover. Shadow's lips were pulled back, his sharp teeth bared. Joshua's eyes gleamed as red as the light from the lantern, and his mouth was open and twisted into an angry grimace.

"Joshua," Amelia stammered, "I — I wanted to clean this cellar, and I — I — "

Joshua opened his mouth wider, but the only sound that came out was a horrible groan.

4

"What did you do?" Chris asked.

"I know what I would have liked to do," Amos said. "I would have liked to kick up my heels and run away from that place as fast as I could."

"But you didn't. Or did you?" Amy asked.

"I didn't," Amos said, "because I was too frightened to move. Amelia's the one who should get credit for bravery."

"Why?" Amy leaned forward eagerly.

"I'll tell you," Amos said, and he rocked back and forth for a few moments before he continued his story.

Amelia stood as tall as she could and looked Joshua straight in the eyes. "It is my job to keep this house tidy and comfortable," she said. "This cellar is part of the house."

"You have no right to touch my money!" Joshua shouted.

"Your money is still your money, and you may

keep it wherever you choose," Amelia said. "I do not want your money, but I do want a clean house." She pointed at the hole the rat had run into. "Without rats in it!"

Joshua's eyes shifted to me, and I felt as though my knees were melted butter and I'd fall over at any minute. "I warned this boy to stay out of the cellar! He disobeyed me!"

"Amos told me of your orders," Amelia said, "but I asked him to come down here to help me. Blame me for his being here, not him." She put a hand on my shoulder and added, "He doesn't want your money, either."

Joshua was in control now. He had calmed down, but his features were still twisted into a ferocious scowl. "I am the only one who has known where my money is hidden."

Amelia fingered the gold chain at her throat. Even in the lantern light I could see two bright spots of red on her cheeks and noticed that her fingers trembled just a little. "As I told you, Joshua, neither Amos nor I want any of your money. You may hide it wherever else you please. We will not look for it, although since I am your wife I would think you would trust me."

Joshua stared at her for a long moment, then grumbled, "I trust no one." He grabbed the sack of money, fastened it, and shoved it back under the stairs. Then he turned to face us. "Never come into this cellar again," he snapped.

He waited while Amelia and I climbed the stairs, Shadow at our heels.

Amelia gave me a little push when we were back in the kitchen. "Go outside and get to work," she whispered.

I was only too glad to get out of the house. My mouth was dry and my hands were clammy. I hurried into my coat and gloves and ran out to the barn.

I worked hard all day, even skipping the noon meal, afraid of seeing Joshua again. It was a strange day, too. The chickens were nervous, suddenly flapping into the air and squawking as though they'd seen a fox. The old horse — I had never heard Joshua call him anything but "Horse" — was skittish, kicking against the boards in his stall. I let him run free in the meadow, but he laid back his ears, whinnied, and galloped in one direction and then another as though he were demented. Even the birds would now and then rise from their perches in the trees in noisy clouds, swooping away like puffs of black smoke. Maybe the animals sensed the danger and fear at the Hanover farm. I didn't understand what was causing their strange behavior.

Amelia called me to come to supper just as darkness began to settle over the land. The air was still, and although the night would again be cold, a strange, warm, sour smell seemed to come from the ground beneath my feet.

Supper was eaten in silence. Of course, Joshua usually didn't speak, but I missed Amelia's usual cheerful chatter. Shadow, who usually lay on the floor near Joshua's feet, prowled the room, whimpering at the door, walking in Amelia's path as she carried our dirty plates from the table to the drainboard.

"Shadow is acting strangely," Amelia said.

"There is nothing wrong with Shadow," Joshua snapped.

I piped up. "All the animals are nervous. I had a hard time catching and stabling the horse tonight. One of the chickens even flew in my face as though she were crazed."

Joshua shook his head. "There would be no reason for the animals to act in such a manner," he said. "You are mistaken."

The man only believed what he wanted to believe. He could only see what he wanted to see. When Amelia invited me to bring a chair closer to the fire, I pulled on my coat instead and told her I was tired and wanted to go to bed early.

My small room in the barn was cold, but I wrapped up well in blankets and soon my body warmth made me cozy and sleepy. The horse stomped and nickered now and then, and the chickens flew up and down from the rafters instead of settling down to sleep, but I was tired enough to push the sounds out of my head and fall asleep.

I remember a dream of a horse running across wide, open fields, and I was on his back. It wasn't Joshua's horse under me. It was a large white animal who could run as fast as the wind blew. But then the horse began to roar with the horrible roaring of thunder, and he threw me from his back so violently that I sailed through the air and smashed against the ground.

Suddenly I awoke. I found myself sprawled against the rough barn wall as though I'd been tossed there like a sack of dried corn. The ground was shaking and heaving, and I tried to hold on. But there was nothing to hold on to. I could actually hear the crunching of rocks deep, deep beneath where I lay, and the groaning of the earth as it shifted. It was the most awful, terrifying noise I had ever heard in my life. It was the noise that nightmares are made of.

The shaking seemed to last forever. Later, someone told me the earthquake was measured in minutes and seconds, and he said that it happened around two in the morning. But during that quake I lost all sense of time.

I acted automatically, without thinking. I untied the horse and opened the barn door so he could escape. It was after I had pushed open the heavy door that I saw the far end of the barn had collapsed, leaving it open to the sky. I ran outside, too, heading for Joshua Hanover's house.

The earth shuddered again, and I staggered, falling flat, staring up at stars and a bright moon that seemed to wobble in the sky. I still lay there after the movement stopped. I think I was waiting for it to begin again.

But when I heard Shadow's frantic barking I sat up, then scrambled to my feet. I was close to the front door of Joshua's house. Most of the house was standing. It was low and solidly built and had moved with the flow of the earth, but a chunk of the roof and some of the bricks in the chimney had fallen and were lying on the ground.

The door suddenly flew open, and Shadow raced outside as though he had gone crazy. Saliva was dripping from his jaws, his eyes were wide and red, and a high-pitched sound, like a scream, came from his open mouth. He tore off toward the woods.

Joshua appeared in the doorway. He was clutching the canvas sack of money. "Shadow!" he yelled at his dog. "Shadow! Come back!"

Shadow either didn't hear him or, for the first time in his life, didn't obey him. Shadow ran on. As he reached the edge of the woods another quake rolled under us. It was lighter than the first two, but strong enough to make me sit down hard on the ground and to topple an old pine that crashed in a shower of dust and needles.

I heard Shadow give a yelp, and wondered if he'd been hit. But then I heard him howl again, and the howl was farther away. He was all right.

Perhaps it was the first time that Joshua had ever been frightened for something or someone else. His face sagged as though it had been stretched down to his chest, and he cried mournfully, "Shadow! Wait! Come back to me!"

He dropped that sack of money by the front door and ran after his dog. He stumbled and fell a couple of times, because the land had been twisted and pulled apart into hillocks and trenches. Between the house and the road the ground had dropped about ten feet, creating a deep trench. Joshua ran next to it, veered to his right, crossed the pasture, and disappeared into the woods.

I immediately began to worry about Amelia. Was she still inside? I ran toward the house, calling her name.

Amelia appeared in the doorway, clutching the doorframe as though she expected to be thrown off her feet at any minute. Her hair was loose around her shoulders, and she wore what ladies called a "wrapper." The gold chain around her neck glimmered in the moonlight.

"Amos!" she cried. "Are you all right?"

"I guess so. Are you?"

"Yes." She nodded as I ran to join her. "Where's Joshua?"

"In the woods." She looked puzzled, so I explained, "He ran after Shadow. Come on, Amelia. We have to get away from here!"

"But where can we go?"

I just shook my head. I didn't know. I had no answer for her.

She still clung to the doorframe. "I'm so frightened!" she whispered. "When will it end?"

"Maybe it's over now," I said.

But Amelia's eyes suddenly widened as she looked over my shoulder. She stiffened and screamed, "Look at the river!"

I turned to see a wall of water veer off from the river, rushing into and filling the trench where the earth had split. The force of the water tore huge chunks of dirt from the sides of the trench. Roaring and churning through this new path, and growing wider by the minute, the river gobbled the land that it swept through.

"We'll drown!" Amelia cried.

"No, we won't!" I shouted. I picked up the sack of money that Joshua had dropped. I pulled Amelia away from the doorway and shoved the sack into her arms. "Run for high ground!" I yelled at her. "Run!"

Amelia did as I said. She ran around the corner

of the house and toward the wooded hill. I started after her, but tripped and sprawled on my face. Something cut a painful gash across my right cheek, and I tried to stop the bleeding with the sleeve of my coat and scramble to my feet at the same time. I fell again.

By the time I managed to pull myself up Amelia was no longer in sight.

"Amelia!" I called, but there was no answer. Amelia had disappeared.

5

"**A**nother quake rolled under my feet," Amos said. "There is nowhere to go when the earth moves violently. There is nothing anyone can do to escape. I lay on the ground, clutching the stump of an uprooted tree. I could hear the earth's deep roar, and the rush of the river, and Joshua's voice screaming through the darkness, 'Shadow! Shadow, come!' Terrified, I hung on to the tree stump until that quake had passed and the earth settled and was still."

Amy gave a long sigh. "Where was Amelia?"

Amos shook his head. "Ah, that is what Joshua and I wanted to know — each for our own reasons. I'll tell you what happened."

We had other quakes during the early-morning hours. Some of them were strong, others were like the gentle shudders that shake a child after a bout of tears. There were many moments, there in the darkness, when I thought that the earth was being destroyed and daylight would never come again, so it was a relief to see the sky turn pale and gray with the first morning light.

The land looked as though giant fingers had dug through it, stirring and poking and slapping it into a new shape. The strangest sight, however, was the river, which had divided to pour around both sides of the farm and hill, turning what was left of Joshua's property into an island. Across the still-churning water I could faintly see some of the buildings of the town. The church had lost its steeple, and I was sure there must be great damage to the houses and stores as well. The river carried odd things past us, moving too fast to beach them. There were whole trees, some of them slamming into each other in midstream. Part of a chest of drawers sailed downstream. Where it came from I couldn't guess. A wooden chair bobbed in the current. It looked as sturdy as when it was new.

I wanted to show these things to Amelia. I had to find her, so I headed toward the woods.

But out of the woods came Joshua. He swayed like a young pine caught in a storm, and he shouted at me, "Where is Amelia?"

"I don't know," I said. "I'm going to look for her."

Joshua's eyes widened, as though he had suddenly thought of something important, and he ran past me as fast as he could go, heading out of the woods and toward the farmhouse. I turned and ran after him.

He stopped when he came to the front of the house and stared at the ground.

"Where is it?" he yelled. "Where is my money?"

"I gave it to Amelia," I said.

He whirled to stare at me. "She took it? Amelia took my money?"

"No," I said. "I put the sack into her hands. I told her to run for high ground."

"She took it," he muttered as though he hadn't heard a word I'd said.

I tried to explain. "It was the river! It split! Half of it left its course and rushed through that trench with a terrible power. We couldn't leave the money on the ground. It might have been swept away. We didn't know how high the new branch of the river would come."

Joshua glared. "The river didn't reach the house."

"We thought it might."

"She took my money!"

"Will you look, Mr. Hanover?" I shouted at him. "Look at the river! It's created an island! How did we know what it would do?"

He slowly turned and looked to both sides. I think it was the first time that he realized what had happened to his property.

I took a good look at the island, too, recognizing the fact that I was marooned here with the angry, crazed Joshua Hanover, and there was no chance to escape.

He held one long arm out and pointed to a spot where the pier had been. There were only the tops of two pilings showing above the rough water. From one of them a single board dangled.

"The boat is gone!" he said.

"It must have been swept away," I answered.

"The boat, my money! Amelia betrayed me!" He paused. "She took my savings and left in the boat."

I gasped. That was the craziest idea I'd ever heard. "She couldn't have done that! Not with the way the river was flowing. There was a high wall of water coming at us, and we ran."

His eyes drilled into mine. "Did you see where Amelia ran?"

"Toward the woods."

"Did you see her go into the woods?"

"No. I fell. Then I tried to get up and fell again. When I finally got to my feet she was nowhere in sight."

"Could she have gone back to the boat?"

I took a deep breath. I was afraid of this man, but I was angry with him for suspecting Amelia. "Mr. Hanover, I know that your wife ran into the woods."

"Then come with me," he said. "We'll search for her."

As we crossed the pasture there were small cracks in the earth from which heat seemed to rise, steaming in the cold air. It was hard to walk at times, because the ground was uneven, but the woods were in worse condition.

Trees had fallen, some of them resting on other trees, balancing precariously, ready to crash to the ground at any moment. There were spots that had sunk, drops of four to ten feet, and we had to be careful not to stumble into them.

We called Amelia's name, and we searched all through the woods. The morning had turned to noon. In spite of the horror of what had happened, my stomach began growling with hunger. Joshua Hanover glanced at me. "Now do you agree that she took my money and fled in my boat?" he asked.

"No," I said. "I can't agree to that."

"Then we will search again," he said.

Even though I was ready to drop, we began to cover the same area.

It didn't go well. Once again tremors shuddered through the earth. I fell, sliding face down into one of the holes. There was a loud crack as a tree, roots already dangling in the daylight, was heaved upward. It landed with an echoing thump across part of the hole I was in.

When the earth stopped moving I dared to raise my head. If I hadn't been lying in the hole the huge old pine might have killed me.

I scrambled out of the hole, my hands slipping, my fingers tearing into open cavities in the porous limestone, using these cavities to pull myself to solid ground.

"We'll be killed if we stay in the woods," I told Joshua, but he just shook his head.

"We will cover all the area we can," he said. "If Amelia took shelter here, we'll find her." So we searched again, while the land settled and resettled under us.

As the earth growled and heaved, and I clung to a small tree, I managed to whisper, "It's the end of the world."

"Not yet," Joshua said. He seemed more furious than ever.

The sun was low in the sky when he finally stopped and said, "We have gone over this ground twice. Are you ready to admit that Amelia has left us here?"

I couldn't do that. But I couldn't keep searching. I was exhausted. I just ducked my head and said the first thing that came to my mind. "What happened to Shadow?"

Joshua looked as though everything else had gone out of his mind. He groaned in pain and said, "Come with me."

He led me to what was left of the barn, where he picked up a shovel. Then I followed him on a track between the pasture and the woods. We went higher and higher until we came close to the top of the hill. Joshua stopped so suddenly I almost fell into him. He stooped and pulled aside some small tree limbs and brush.

There lay Shadow.

"We'll dig a grave," Joshua said. "At the edge of the woods, so he will have shade, near the pasture where he loved to run."

I couldn't say a word. I felt sorry for Mr. Hanover, but at the same time I had been afraid of Shadow. I was glad I'd never have to be afraid of him again.

Joshua dug the grave, while I stood aside. I could see down the meadow to the new branch of the river, and across it the faint lights that were being lit in the town. With all my heart I wished I were there and not on the island.

Without a word Joshua went back into the woods and picked up Shadow's body. He carried it to the grave and laid it down gently. He shoveled the dirt back into the grave and smoothed down the top.

I don't know what I expected. I thought maybe he'd say a few nice words about Shadow or tell me some good story he remembered about something Shadow had done. But instead, he didn't seem to see me. He looked out over the rise, back to the house and to the spot where the pier and boat had been. His complexion grew darker, and his eyes glowed red in the dim evening light. His face seemed to swell, and it looked to me as though he'd grown even taller. He clenched his fists and raised them high in the air, shaking them furiously.

"I loved her, and she betrayed me!" he shouted so suddenly that I stepped backward and stumbled, tripping over a log and falling on my back. "I will have vengeance!"

He turned around and stomped back into the woods, leaving me alone with Shadow's grave, the still-grumbling earth, and the rushing darkness.

6

Amy bounced in her rocking chair, making it squeak against the floorboards of the porch. "Didn't anyone rescue you?" she asked.

"Don't be dumb," Chris said. "He's here, isn't he?"

"Of course," Amy said. "That was dumb. Sorry."

"My story's not over," Amos said. "Some of it has to do with what happened after the rescue."

"Tell us." Chris hugged his knees, eager to hear the rest. "We're ready."

Mr. Corley rocked silently for a few moments. Then he began to speak.

I didn't like being cooped up on that island with Joshua Hanover, I can tell you that! I knew that no search parties could be sent until the river had quieted. The water still churned, and the currents were strong.

I managed to repair part of the barn. The horse never showed up again. What happened to him,

I'll never know. So I had the barn to myself. I didn't go near the house, except to get some food when Joshua wasn't around. He prowled the island, striding down the beach with his head down and his hands clasped behind his back. Sometimes I'd see him loping across the pasture and into the woods. He never spoke to me. It was as though he didn't see me or know I was there.

But something saw me. I'd get the feeling at times that something was watching me, and I'd turn quickly, but no one was ever there. A couple of times at night, from the direction of the woods, I could hear a dog howling. I knew there was no dog on the island, so I'd scrunch down under the blanket, wadding it against my ears so I couldn't hear.

And sometimes late in the night, another sound would carry across the darkness like a cold breeze. From somewhere on the island Joshua would be angrily crying into the night, "Vengeance! I will have vengeance!"

I thought about Amelia often. I even walked the island myself, searching for any trace of her. Maybe she *had* taken the boat and escaped. I hoped with all my heart that she had, even though I couldn't imagine how such a small boat could stay afloat on that turbulent river.

I hung a torn shirt on a tree near the new branch of the river, hoping people in town would see it and recognize it as a signal for help, but Joshua spied it and tugged it down, tossing it into the churning river.

The quakes went on and on for days. Once they had started, they couldn't seem to stop. Every few hours there was a new movement of the earth. Some were light enough to tolerate, and some were strong jolts. I wondered, during this time, if I would live to see the end of them.

But after a couple of weeks the earth quieted down, and the river finally settled to a normal flow. Eventually, as soon as they could do it in safety, some of the people in town sent out a boat to rescue us. I was never so glad to see anybody in my whole life!

I jumped up and down along the riverbank, waving and shouting, as the boat arrived. And I ran into the icy water, helping to pull it ashore and beach it. I recognized some of the men who had come. One was Mr. Taylor, the banker, and one was Mr. Owens, who owned the dry goods store.

"We'll take you and the Hanovers to town, Amos," Mr. Taylor said. He glanced up at the house. Joshua had done nothing to try to repair it. "It looks as though you had a bad time of it here."

"Bad time all over," Mr. Owens added. "Folks have got lots of repair work to do in town. Whole back end of my store went down in the first shock."

They went on about some of the damage and how most of the people had lived through the earthquakes, shaking their heads over the few who hadn't.

Finally Mr. Taylor asked, "Where are the Hanovers?"

So I told him about Amelia's disappearance and how Joshua just roamed the island looking for her.

"We'd better take him back with us," Mr. Owens said. "He can't stay on here. His property's completely cut off now by the river."

"We'll have to find him," I answered. "He's probably in the woods."

"Is that mean dog with him?" Mr. Owens asked.

"He's dead," I said, and shivered. I didn't want to talk about Shadow's grave and the howling in the night. I just wanted to get away from this island as fast as I could.

There were five men, and they divided up into two groups to go looking for Joshua. Two men went along the riverbank, and two went toward the woods. One man stayed with the boat. I went with Mr. Owens and Mr. Taylor, who headed across the pasture and into the woods. In the distance I could hear the other men calling Joshua's name. We called, too, but he didn't answer.

So many trees had fallen that it was hard to make our way through the piney woods. We had to watch out for soft places and spots where the ground had dropped.

"I had a horse once who broke a leg stepping through the top of one of these old limestone caves." Mr. Owens grumbled and puffed as he skirted a deep hole and climbed over a fallen tree.

"Why doesn't Joshua answer us?" Mr. Taylor asked. He stopped and took a couple of deep breaths. "Do you suppose he's got himself hurt and is lying somewhere, needing help?"

I had to say it. "I think we might find him near Shadow's grave."

I led them toward the top edge of the woods, where the pines met the meadow, and where Joshua had buried Shadow. Sure enough, there he was, standing still and looking out over the river. Joshua could see the boat. He must have heard the shouting of his name. He had to know we were looking for him.

Mr. Owens, who was out of breath, was impatient. "Joshua," he said, "didn't you hear all the ruckus we were making, trying to find you?"

Joshua didn't speak. He just slowly turned and stared at Mr. Owens. In the late sunlight Joshua's eyes were wide and red and angry.

Mr. Owens took a step backward. He looked a little scared of Joshua, but he said, "We've been spending a lot of time searching for you."

"I didn't ask you to come," Joshua said.

Mr. Taylor tried to smooth things over. "We came to help you."

"I don't need your help."

"Joshua, your house is damaged. You're cut off from the town. You'll need — "

Joshua thundered at him, "I don't need anything from the town or from you! Get off my property!"

Mr. Taylor didn't want to give up. "Won't you please come with us, Joshua?"

"No! Get out of here! This land belongs to me, and I'm never going to leave it!"

Mr. Owens tugged at Mr. Taylor's coat sleeve. "Come on, Jim," he said.

"But he can't stay here by himself."

"He's in no mood to come with us now. We can try again later."

Joshua raised his fists, waving them in the air, and groaned so loudly that his body shuddered. Mr. Taylor, Mr. Owens, and I scurried across the pasture back to the beach as fast as we could go. The other search party had returned, so Mr. Taylor explained everything to them. We all climbed into the boat and rowed to the town.

It was a terrifying time. Just as repair work was well underway, another series of earthquakes hit. They began toward the end of January, and when people thought the worst was over, the quakes came again, toward the end of the first week of February. From that horrible moment on December 12, until the February quakes were over, hundreds of earthquakes took place. No one could believe what was happening. It wasn't real. It was like a nightmare that wouldn't end.

Everyone in town worked night and day trying to make repairs and to take care of each other. There was so much to do and think about that we all forgot about Joshua Hanover, until one day in late February, Mr. Taylor got together some men to row to the island to see if Joshua needed or wanted help.

I didn't go. I didn't want to see him again. But I was curious enough to be waiting at the dock when the men returned.

Joshua wasn't with them.

"He wouldn't come?" I was astonished.

"He *couldn't* come," Mr. Taylor said. "Joshua Hanover is dead. We found his body lying across the grave he had made for his dog. The place you showed us, Amos. We buried him there."

Amos Corley was silent for a few moments. Then he said, "No one returned to the island for many years, until — "

He paused again, and Chris asked, "Until what?"

"Until some of us began talking about what happened during that quake and about Amelia and — " His voice drifted off.

"And what?"

"I was older," Amos said. "By this time I was a young man. I'd made a place for myself in town and was working for Mr. Owens in his store. Maybe I was a bit foolish, but one night, when I was with some friends, I began to tell everything that had happened on the island, things I had kept to myself, which I had never mentioned before."

Harvey Owens, son of the man who had hired me, leaned forward eagerly. "Amos," he said. "You're telling us that Joshua Hanover really did keep his money in a canvas sack."

"That's what I said. I saw it. I held it."

"And you handed it to his wife and saw her run toward the woods with it."

"That's right."

"I remember the river that night of the earthquake," he said. "It was wild. For a while the river even ran backward. She couldn't have taken that sack of money into a small rowboat and survived."

"I don't think she did. I think the wall of water tore the boat away when it destroyed the pier."

"The bag of money was heavy. Right?" Harvey asked.

"Yes."

"So if Amelia Hanover wanted to escape, whether she took the boat or not, she probably didn't try to carry that heavy canvas bag with her."

"I suppose not," I said. It made sense.

"So the bag of money must be somewhere on the island."

"We searched and searched. We couldn't find Amelia or the money."

"You didn't look in the right places. You searched where Joshua searched."

"What are you getting at?" I asked Harvey.

Harvey sat back and grinned. "A treasure hunt. Somewhere on that island is a bag of money! Let's find it!"

Everybody got excited about it — except me. The idea of setting foot on that island again terrified me, but I didn't want my friends to know it, so I agreed.

We planned it for the next day, because it was Saturday, but we all had jobs to do, so it was late in the afternoon before we climbed into a boat and rowed to the island.

The day was quiet and warm, and the afternoon sun laid a soft glow over Joshua Hanover's meadow. The grasses were overgrown and ragged, and a deathly silence covered the island like a blanket. There wasn't even a bird to be heard. I could tell that the others felt almost as nervous as I did.

"Shush!" someone whispered. "Listen."

But there was nothing to hear.

Harvey spoke up bravely. "There's no point in

standing around here. Tell us, Amos. In which direction did Amelia Hanover run?"

I pointed up the meadow, toward the woods. Harvey started out, and the rest of us followed. With each step I felt worse about what we were doing, and I began to have that strange sensation again that something was watching me.

We were almost at the edge of the woods when we heard a cry that frightened us into statues. None of us could move. We could only stare ahead at the edge of the woods as a maddened black dog raced forth. Behind him rose the ghost of a tall, gaunt man whose eyes blazed with fire. He raised his fists high into the air, glared at us, and shouted, "Vengeance!"

7

"Is that really true?" Amy huddled into the rocker and wrapped her arms around herself, as though the ghosts were on this porch.

"Of course it's true," Amos said.

"What did you do when you saw the ghosts?"

"We turned and ran as fast as we could down to the boat. A few years later someone else tried to hunt for the treasure on the island, but came back frightened and trembling and reported seeing the ghosts of Joshua Hanover and Shadow. No one ever set foot on the island again."

Chris spoke up. "I don't believe anyone saw a ghost. I think people heard the stories and were scared and imagined what they saw."

"Believe what you will," Amos said.

Chris thought a moment. "Do you really think the sack of coins is there?"

"It's not up to me to say."

"I'd like to go to the island," Chris said.

"No!" Amy said.

"Yes!" Chris turned to Amy. "Don't you see? This is our chance to prove the stories are just old superstitions. We can look around the island and get some ideas for Aunt Jennie, so she can make it into a picnic area. When we come back and report that the island is a great place to visit — without a ghost in sight — people won't be afraid to visit the island. Aunt Jennie could carry out her plans for the inn."

"Well, maybe," Amy said.

"Besides," Chris said. "What if we find the sack of money? That would help Aunt Jennie pay her bills."

"I think you should go," Amos told them. His eyes shone with eagerness. "It's time for the ghosts to be laid to rest."

Their mother called from inside the house, "Chris! Amy! It's getting late!"

"I'll take you to the island if you like," Amos said.

Chris got to his feet. "Yes!" he said. "When?"

"Be at the dock in town tomorrow morning before five o'clock."

"That's awfully early," Amy said.

"We'll be there," Chris said. "Before five. And thanks. Thanks for telling us the story."

"Hey, you two, where are you?" their mother

called. "It's too dark to be out there."

"Coming!" Amy called. She and Chris hurried into the house.

Their mother and Aunt Jennie were in the downstairs bathroom, struggling with a strip of wallpaper. "This is a small room," Aunt Jennie said. "We haven't got enough space to maneuver. We need the two of you to get in here and put this strip of paper in that tiny alcove behind the door."

As they squeezed around each other, changing places, Chris said, "We were on the porch, talking to Amos Corley."

"Who's Amos Corley?" Aunt Jennie asked.

"Doesn't he work for you?"

"I don't think so. Of course, I don't know the names of all the workmen who've been here. But what is he doing on the back porch so late in the evening?" She immediately walked to the back door, opened it, and looked out. "No one's on the porch," she said.

"He probably left when we came inside," Chris said.

"He told us about the big earthquake," Amy said. "You know, the one when the river split and made your island."

"That was a terrible quake," Aunt Jennie said. "I've read about it. It went on and on for three months. It was the worst quake ever to take place in the United States."

"I remember reading about that earthquake, too," their mother said. "In fact, I think you gave me the magazine article." She turned to Amy and Chris. "That first earthquake was so violent that the shock waves were felt as far away as Boston!"

"Wow!" Chris said. "Amos told us how awful it felt to be in it." He ran the brush over the strip of wallpaper, checking to see that it was perfectly straight.

"He must have read about it, too," Aunt Jennie said.

"No. He was there," Chris said. He squeezed out of the bathroom and wiped the paste from his hands to his jeans. "He was living on the island — before it became an island — when the quakes took place."

"He couldn't have been," their mother said. She began picking up the bucket and tools they'd been using.

"Why not?" Chris asked.

"Because the quakes took place during December of 1811 and the first two months of 1812, that's why."

"The room looks great, kids. Thanks for your help," Aunt Jennie said. She and Liz went toward the kitchen to clean up.

"I don't understand this," Amy said to Chris. "If Amos was thirteen in 1811, that would make him practically two hundred years old! He couldn't be that old!"

Chris shrugged. "He was telling a good story, and just put himself into it. He didn't think we'd ask anyone about the date of the earthquake."

"You mean he was just trying to scare us?" Amy stood up straighter. "Well, we'll show him we don't believe in his crazy old ghosts."

Chris chuckled. "We'll go with him tomorrow to the island. It will give us a chance to prove that the island isn't haunted. But don't let on to him that we know the truth." He poked Amy on the shoulder. "And don't tell anyone that we're going. We'll have a great surprise for Aunt Jennie!"

Amy giggled. "This is going to be fun."

But the next morning, so early there was a gray mist over the river, it didn't seem to be fun. Chris and Amy got up early and sneaked out of the house to find the ground still soggy from the week of heavy rain. The summer air wasn't as hot and sticky as it would be later in the day, so Amy wore a sweater over her T-shirt and jeans. Chris was also wearing a cotton shirt with his jeans, and both of them wore sneakers.

Amos was waiting for them, so Chris and Amy

greeted him and climbed into Amos's old battered rowboat.

Amos wasn't as talkative as he had been the night before, which was all right with Chris. It was too early and quiet to talk. Amy sat huddled against Chris, her sweater wrapped tightly around her. Now and then she'd shiver. Their feet were wet, and the water in the bottom of the boat seemed to be growing deeper.

"The boat's leaking," Chris told Amos.

Amos handed Chris a large, rusty tin can. "It's an old boat. Won't last much longer. Better bail out some of that water."

"Is it far?" Chris asked. He worked hard, but it didn't help. The boat was sinking fast.

Chris tried to peer ahead through the fog. They were slowly and steadily getting close to the island. He could hear wavelets slapping the beach, and now and then he could see the dark outlines of the tops of the pines.

Suddenly Amos lifted the oars, resting them on the sides of the boat in their locks. "We're almost on the island," he said. "Just a few more feet, and you can beach the boat."

"Thank goodness!" Amy whispered.

"This is as far as I can go with you," Amos said.

"What do you mean?" Chris asked.

But Amos answered, "You have a job to do.

You must put the ghosts to rest."

Before Amy or Chris could move or speak, Amos began to slowly dissolve. Chris reached out a hand to clutch him, to hold him, but Amos was no longer there. For an instant only his eyes remained, two bright spots staring through the mist.

8

Amy screamed, "Chris!" and grabbed her brother around the neck. The old rowboat rocked wildly.

Chris tried to pry loose her fingers. "Stop it, Amy! We'll end up in the water!" He managed to pull free and crossed into Amos's seat. "Come on over here, Amy! Take one of the oars! Hurry up!"

Amy did as she was told, shivering all the while. "We've got to row back, Chris," she said.

"We can't," he told her as he pulled on his oar. "The boat won't make it. It's shot — we've got to touch land before it sinks."

Amy tugged at her oar, and the boat began to swing erratically. "We can't go to that island!"

"We have to. Pull! Harder!" Chris timed his stroke to Amy's, so the boat would stay on course.

Amy sniffled. "I'm scared, Chris."

"So am I," he said.

"Amos was a ghost."

"I know."

"You said you didn't believe in ghosts. You said — "

The boat stopped with a lurch that threw them forward. Amy dropped her oar with a splash.

"We touched land," Chris said. He stood and turned, facing the island. The early morning light sifted through the mists, illuminating a narrow beach that divided the water from the woods. A breeze rustled the pines that apparently had taken over much of the island.

Amy tugged her sweater into place and folded her arms. "I'm going to stay right here," she said.

"You can't," Chris said. "Come on. Just a few steps, and we'll be on dry land."

"My feet will get wet."

"They're already wet." He held out a hand. "Amy, we've got to stick together."

She stood up reluctantly, gingerly stepping out of the boat and into the shallow water. She followed Chris onto the beach.

Chris studied the beach. "People could come here for cookouts. It's pretty. Aunt Jennie could get a dock built right about where we're standing, and maybe she'd want to clear out a few trees."

"What's the matter with you?" Amy asked. "We just got scared to death by a ghost, and you talk about cookouts!"

"I'm trying not to think about Amos," Chris said.

"He's all I *can* think about." Amy shivered again. "I wish the sun would come out. That would help."

Chris glanced at the sky. "It probably won't. Look. The sky is overcast."

"More rain. That's all we need," Amy grumbled. "Why did Amos bring us here? What did he want?"

"He told us it was time to put the ghosts to rest," Chris said.

"That doesn't mean anything."

"It must have meant something to Amos. I guess we'll have to figure it out."

"We don't have to figure it out. We just have to get off this island."

"How are we going to do that?"

Amy thought a minute. "We can send a signal. Remember that Amos said he had hung a torn shirt where people in town could see it. We could hang up something."

"What?"

"My sweater?" Amy sighed. "It wouldn't be big enough to see, would it? No, it wouldn't. It will have to be something bigger. But what? I don't know."

"If you stop having a conversation with yourself and listen for a minute, I'll tell you my idea," Chris said. "We can build a bonfire."

"Do you know how?" Amy asked.

"Of course I do," he said. "Learning how was part of that wilderness expedition I went on. We can gather up some of the pine branches that have fallen from the trees and pine needles and whatever else we can find. We'll make a huge bonfire."

Amy ran to the edge of the pines and picked up a small branch. "Look! There's lots of stuff in here under the trees."

"Just one thing," Chris said. "We'll have to find something to light the fire with."

"Oh," Amy said. "Like matches." She sat on the damp ground and rested her chin in her hands. "We won't find matches in a place like this."

"We might find something else," Chris said. "Amos spoke about a lantern. They had to have oil or kerosene or something for the lantern, and they had to have something to light it." He paused and looked at Amy. "We'll just look through the Hanovers' house and see what we come up with."

"Oh, no!" Amy said. "There's no way I'm going inside the Hanovers' house."

"It won't be so bad," Chris told her. "We could see part of a roof and chimney, so some of it must still be standing. It's just a small house. We can look through it and get out quickly."

"No," Amy said.

"Then I'll look through it and you can stay here."

"No!" she said. "I don't want to stay by myself."

"Would you rather live here on the beach until someone just happens to look at the island with binoculars or thinks of searching for us on the island? No one knew we were coming here!"

Amy looked as though she was going to cry. "We'll be okay, Amy," Chris said quickly. "Let's build the stack for the bonfire first. Then we can talk about looking through the house."

He began to drag small dried logs and branches from under the trees to the open beach. He held one up to Amy. "Look at this one. It's full of pitch."

"What's pitch?"

"It's the sap from pine trees. It burns like kerosene. It will make a great fire."

"Do all the branches have it?"

"No. Just some. Look for the ones with these brown and yellowish bumps on them. That's what pitch looks like."

Amy and Chris worked hard, and the pile began to grow larger.

In spite of being overcast, the day rapidly became warmer. Amy tossed her sweater on the ground and stood back, studying the growing mound of branches. "Is this big enough?" she asked.

"Not yet," Chris said. "We might have to keep the fire going for quite a while until someone notices it."

"Chris, I just thought of something," she said. "No one's going to spot the fire during the daylight."

"I know," Chris said. "I'm going to light it tonight, after dark."

Amy looked nervously over her shoulder. "You mean we'll have to be here all day?"

"Have you got a better idea? Come on. Let's keep this pile growing." Chris led the way back into the woods.

Inside the thick pine grove the light was murky, with a greenish cast, and the air was damp. The ground under their feet was soggy and spongy with layers of pine needles. They worked hard, building the mound for the bonfire higher and higher, but each trip led them further into the woods.

"This pile of wood is as high as our heads," Amy complained. "Isn't this enough?"

"One more trip," Chris said, and headed back into the forest.

"There's a log over here," Amy said, and she ran past him to reach it. "Help me carry it." She bent to pick up one end of the log.

Chris joined her, but didn't stoop to help. "Look at that, Amy," he whispered, as he stared through the trees at a small clearing.

She stepped up behind him and clutched his arm. "Look at what?" She whispered, too, and her voice was trembling.

"The house! The farm! There it is!"

Pines had grown into the clearing around the

house, but the pasture remained. It stretched up the hill, its long grasses, yellowed from the mid-day heat of summer, rippling in the breeze. At the foot of the pasture, near the house, lay a pile of weathered, rotting boards that must have once been part of the barn.

Directly in front of them was the house itself, its front door hanging open as though beckoning them to come inside. It was a small frame house. Once it must have been painted, but now its boards were so streaked with dirt and black mildew that it was impossible to know what color the house had once been. The wood shingles on the roof were split and curled, and a large hole gaped at one side where a section of roof had fallen in.

Something suddenly fluttered at one of the narrow windows, and Chris jumped. Amy gasped.

"It's okay," Chris said, glad that Amy didn't know how fast his heart was beating. "It's just a faded old piece of a curtain. The breeze must have moved it."

"Let's go back to the beach," Amy whispered.

Chris squared his shoulders. "Why are we whispering? There's no one on the island to hear us."

"In case you haven't noticed," Amy said, "there's *nothing* on this island, not even a bird! It's so quiet it's creepy!"

"You're right," Chris said. "There's nothing here but us, so we're just scaring ourselves. The best thing we could do right now is to look inside that house and find something to set off our bonfire, so we'll be ready to give our signal as soon as it's dark."

"We'll just look and come right out. Promise?"

"You call it," Chris said. "We'll leave when you say so."

"Okay then," Amy said, "but you go first."

Chris hesitated on the doorstep and looked inside the house. The room was dim, yet daylight entered through a large hole in the roof near the back of the main room. He could see the kitchen beyond the living room. There was probably a bedroom off to the side. The inside walls of the house had once been white, according to Amos, but now they were streaked with rain and dirt. An overstuffed chair, its fabric deteriorated into shreds, stood by a large stone fireplace. Some squat wooden chairs and a table rested solidly on the floor, which was layered with dirt and pine needles. An oil lamp lay in jagged pieces under the window, and broken flowerpots littered the room.

Chris stepped inside, stumbling over a square wooden box, which broke apart, spilling a small yellow bundle on the floor.

Amy bent and touched it with the tips of her fingers. "It's slick. It feels funny," she said. "What is this, Chris?"

Chris picked it up. "It's an oiled cloth," he answered. "It's wrapped around something." As he spoke he unwrapped the cloth and pulled out a book. He dropped the cloth and opened the book. "It's a diary, I think," he said.

"Amelia's?" Amy eagerly pulled the book from his hands, and a page fluttered out. She stooped to pick it up. "A drawing!" she said.

It was a small drawing of a young woman. It looked as though it had been done in pencil, and the paper was yellowed and fragile. The woman had large eyes, and a solemn expression. Her hair was pulled back tightly, and her dress was plain, with only a small collar. Around her neck a thin, twisted necklace had been drawn.

"The gold chain!" Amy cried. "It has to be Amelia!" She handed the picture to Chris and looked through the book. "It's like a journal," she said. "Here — Amelia writes about her daily life in Boston before she married Joshua. Oh, Chris, I can't wait to read this! I bet she had this by the door ready to take with her."

"You can read it later," Chris said. "Let's look for something we can use to light the bonfire."

Amy carefully tucked the picture back inside the journal. They walked across what must have been the main room, or living room, to the room that was probably the kitchen, and stopped to glance around at the crumbling wreckage inside the house.

The terrible silence of the island seemed to wrap itself around them.

"I don't like being alone in here," Amy murmured.

"I don't think we *are* alone," Chris whispered. "I have this feeling that someone is watching us."

9

"**D**on't say things like that!" Amy took a step closer to Chris and clutched Amelia's journal tightly.

"Don't you feel it?"

They paused, and as they listened the silence was broken by the sound of something moving in the room they had left.

"Let's get out of here!" Amy cried.

"We haven't got what we need!" Chris said. He whirled back to the doorway between the two rooms, staring into the living room of the house. "There's no one here, Amy. It must have been an animal that we heard."

"What kind of animal?"

"I don't know. Maybe a — " Chris stopped.

"Go on. Say it," Amy demanded. "You were going to say 'maybe a rat,' weren't you? Well, I don't want to stay in a house with a rat any more than I want to stay in a house with a ghost! Let's go!"

"In a minute," Chris said. There was a cupboard at one side of the room, and he threw open the doors. Inside was a jumble of pots and bowls, many of them broken. "Nothing here," he said.

"Then we haven't got a reason for staying here."

Chris turned and examined the rest of the kitchen. Nearby stood a door. "The cellar's down there," he said.

"You're not going into the cellar," Amy said.

"Yes, I am," Chris told her. "I have to find something."

"Joshua Hanover didn't want anyone in his cellar!"

"Don't get so excited. He didn't want anyone down there, because that's where he kept his money. But the money isn't there anymore." He added, "For that matter, neither is Joshua Hanover."

Chris tugged at the door, which was warped and hard to budge.

"I'm not going down there with you," Amy said.

"You don't have to."

The door suddenly gave, flying open so suddenly that Chris staggered backward.

"You haven't got a flashlight. You won't be able to see anything down there."

But Chris was already on the stairs. "There's enough light from the room to see some of the cellar. It's not very big."

Chris guessed that the cellar was about the size of the house. Much of it was in darkness, but he was able to see the section near the stairs. The room had been cut from the earth, with wooden cross supports against the walls. They were covered with mildew. Patches of damp, dark moss splattered the walls, and the cellar smelled sour and wet. The wooden stairs seemed to be still sturdy, although they wobbled a little when Chris tried them.

"What's in the cellar?" Amy asked.

"Come and look."

"No," Amy said, but Chris heard her move down a few stairs behind him.

Near his feet he heard a rustling noise. He quickly looked toward the sound and saw two small bright eyes. In a flash they were gone. Rats! He hoped Amy hadn't noticed.

"There are some shelves on the wall near the stairs," he said, trying to keep his voice steady, "but they're empty. A lot of the stuff that was kept down here must have been knocked to the floor during the earthquakes. There's broken stuff all over the floor."

"What are you looking for?" Amy asked.

"A small metal box," he said, and held his fingers apart just a few inches. "About so big."

"You mean like this one?"

Chris quickly turned and looked at the spot to

which Amy was pointing. At eye level, directly opposite the kitchen door, was a niche in the wall. Inside the niche was wedged a small, rectangular box. Chris eagerly rushed up the stairs, grabbed it, and opened it. "I found it!" he said.

"You mean *I* found it," Amy said. She stepped back into the kitchen, and Chris followed her. "You still haven't told me what it is."

"It's a tinder box," he said.

"What's a tinder box?"

"I read about them when I was working on my pioneer project. The museum even has one on exhibit. There's a piece of flint and a piece of steel inside. People would rub the flint and steel together to make sparks, and the sparks would catch on kindling and start a fire."

"You're smarter than I thought you were." Amy grinned at Chris. "Now, can we get out of this awful house? You promised that when I said we should go, we'd go, and I've been saying it and saying it."

"I keep my promises," Chris said. "We'll go back to the beach right now." He tucked the box into a pocket of his jeans.

Amy ran to pick up the oiled paper and wrapped the journal tightly. "Poor Amelia," she said. "I wonder what happened to you."

The house suddenly trembled as though caught in a rush of wind.

Amy and Chris stared at each other, then scrambled to get out the front door.

"Something heard us," Amy whispered, looking back at the house.

"It was just the wind," Chris said.

The air was still and damp. "What wind?" Amy asked.

Before Chris could answer, a mournful cry drifted down from the top of the hill. "Shadow! Here, Shadow! Come!"

"Joshua Hanover!" Chris said.

"Run!" Amy yelled.

Chris raced through the woods, stumbling and tripping and bouncing off the trees until he reached the beach. He flung himself down on the ground next to the pile of branches they had made.

"Maybe we won't have to wait until tonight to light this," he said. "Maybe we should set it off right now."

Amy didn't answer, so he said, "What do you think? Will they see the bonfire back at the inn?"

He turned to look at Amy. "Well?"

But Amy wasn't there.

Chris jumped to his feet. "Amy? Where are you? Amy!"

He hurried back to the route they'd taken through the woods, retracing his steps toward the Hanovers' house. "Amy," he called. He shuddered. What had happened to Amy?

He made his way between two trees, and skirted a fallen tree. "Amy!"

"Chris!" The hiss came from behind the large log. "Over here! Be quiet!"

Chris stretched to look over the log and saw his sister huddled against the fallen branches.

"What are you doing there?" he asked.

"Get back here with me! Quick!" she whispered again, adding, "And be quiet!"

Chris crawled over the log, dropping beside her. "Why didn't you run to the beach with me?"

"You were faster than I was. I thought I'd better hide."

"From what? Joshua Hanover? We heard him up at the top of the hill."

Amy shook her head. "I don't know from what. There was something close behind us. It was catching up."

"Did you see it?"

"No. But I knew it was there."

The close-growing pines seemed to cut out much of the morning light. "I didn't see anything," Chris said. "And I'd feel safer in the open than I do in this forest."

"But what about whatever was chasing us?"

"I didn't see anything, and I was yelling for you and making a lot of noise. If something were trying to catch us, it would have found me in a hurry."

Chris stood up and held out a hand to Amy. "Come on. I'd rather be on the beach."

"And I'd rather be back at the inn," Amy said, but she took his hand and got to her feet. She brushed pine needles from her shirt and jeans and looked around cautiously.

"Want to race back?" Chris asked. The damp silence in the woods made him edgy.

"No. I want to walk quietly and carefully."

"It will take longer."

"I'm not kidding, Chris." Amy's expression was solemn. "I want to be able to hear whatever might be near us."

"I'm sorry — " Chris started to say, for the first time feeling guilty that he had been so eager to come to the island that he had talked Amy into it.

"Shhhh," Amy said, interrupting him. "Don't talk. Just listen."

She held the journal tightly, and together they carefully walked through the forest on their way to the beach.

Chris let out a huge sigh of relief as they broke through the trees onto the strip of beach, and Amy said, "We made it!" But she suddenly grabbed Chris's hand so tightly that it hurt. "Chris! What happened to our pile of wood for the bonfire?"

The wood, which had been so carefully stacked

and made ready for the fire, had been scattered.

Chris ran forward and kicked at the nearest pine branch. "Who did this?" he shouted.

"We'll have to put it all back together!" Amy said. "And it was so much hard work in the first place!"

Chris groaned. "We haven't got a choice. Let's get back to work."

Just then a low growl came from the edge of the woods. They whirled to stare. There, standing in the path they had made, was a huge black dog. His lips were pulled back from his teeth in a snarl. He took a step toward them.

10

"**D**on't move!" Chris murmured. The dog took one step and stopped. The stiff hair on its neck bristled as it growled low in its throat.

Carefully, slowly, while keeping his eyes on the dog, Chris bent and picked up a pine branch that was about three feet long with brittle clusters of needles at one end. It was splattered with small lumps of pitch. "Hold this," Chris said to Amy.

From his pocket he pulled the tinder box and opened it. The dog raised his head and moved a step closer to them. It stared into Chris's eyes.

Chris held the flint and steel under the dried needles on the branch and quickly struck them together. Sparks flew, the needles and pitch caught, and fire suddenly blazed, turning the branch into a torch.

Chris dropped the flint and steel and grabbed the branch. He ran toward the dog, holding the branch ahead of him. "Get out of here, Shadow!" he shouted. "Go away!"

Like an echo, far up the hill, a cry came. "Shadow! Come!"

Instantly the dog disappeared.

Amy plopped down. "I've never been so scared in my life. My legs won't hold me up."

"While you're down there, will you pick up the flint and steel for me?" Chris asked.

"Thanks for the sympathy," Amy said.

"I was scared, too," Chris said. He stuck the unlit end of the torch in the sand. The blaze had lasted only a few seconds, but the end of the branch continued to burn.

Amy put the flint and steel in the tinder box and handed it to Chris. "Shadow was going to attack us."

Chris looked toward the woods where Shadow had appeared. "I don't think ghosts can attack people."

"What makes you think that?"

"Well, ghosts don't have bodies. They're just — just — whatever ghosts are made out of."

Amy dusted off the seat of her jeans. "That doesn't sound like a good scientific explanation."

"Trust me," Chris said. "Shadow can't attack you. He'll just appear or disappear, but he can't do anything physical."

Amy spread her arms wide. "Then how about this mess? He was able to do this to the wood we'd collected for our bonfire."

Chris thought a minute. Then he said, "Maybe Amos did it."

"Amos told us he couldn't go to the island with us. It couldn't have been Amos. And besides," Amy said, "Amos is a ghost, too."

"Why would Shadow do it? He'd want to get rid of us."

"It's pretty obvious," Amy said, "that whoever did it doesn't want us to leave."

"So we have to find out why," Chris said.

"I just want to get off this island. I don't want to find out."

"Finding out may be our only answer to getting off the island."

"How are we going to do that?"

Chris glanced at Amy. "You aren't going to like my idea, but I think we ought to go to the Hanovers' house and look around again."

"You're right. I don't like it. I hate it." Amy shook her head. "The house was a mess of broken stuff. The only thing we found that was important was this journal. Besides, to get to the house we have to go back through that creepy woods."

"It isn't a very big woods."

"I won't do it," Amy said.

"Maybe we can go around it," Chris offered. "Let's walk along the water's edge and see if there's some sort of break in the woods."

Amy scowled. "I guess I'll agree to that. But

83

you have to promise we won't go into the woods."

"You can call it," Chris said. "We won't go into the woods unless you say so."

"I've heard *that* before."

Chris glanced at the small bundle in Amy's hand. "Why don't you leave that journal here?"

"Something might happen to it."

"It's wrapped in that oiled paper. Even if it rains it will be protected. Why don't you wedge it in a branch of a tree?"

"Because," Amy said firmly, "I want to take it with me." She looked at the sky. "The clouds are so yucky and dark, it looks like it's going to rain again any minute." She tucked the wrapped journal under the belt on her jeans. "Okay," she said, "I'm ready to go."

Chris picked up the torch.

"Your torch is still burning," Amy said. "That's great! We can take it with us."

"The pitch will keep the wood burning," Chris said. "But pine burns fast. The torch won't last much longer. It's not worth taking." He turned it and stuck it upside down in the sand, snuffing out the glow.

Chris walked along the shore in a southeasterly direction. Amy was right on his heels. At times a lone pine grew right at the water's edge, and they had to climb and scramble over and around it. The shoreline was rocky, and twice Amy stumbled.

Chris jumped from a rock to a patch of flat land that created a small cove. He heard a splash and Amy's shout.

"That does it!" she said. "Now I've scraped my elbow on that rock!" She sat down on the ground, pulled a tissue out of her pocket, and wadded it against her elbow.

Chris bent to examine the wound. "I'm sorry, Amy," he said. "Is it bleeding very much?"

"No," Amy said, "but it stings. How far do we have to go?"

Chris leaned back against the embankment, which was as high as his shoulders. He was sorry Amy had hurt her elbow, but he was glad for a chance to rest a moment. "Not too far," he said.

"I don't mind being here by the water," she said, as she twisted to examine her elbow. "But I don't like the woods. I get the feeling there are things in the woods — like bugs and whatever else lives in the woods — rats? Skunks?" Amy looked up at Chris and the edge of the woods beyond him. She dropped the tissue she'd been holding, and her mouth opened wide.

"Oh!" she whispered. "Chris, don't move!"

"What — " he started to ask, but Amy slowly got to her feet.

"Don't talk! Don't make a sound!" she said. "There's a snake up there on the ground near your head. I don't know if he's poisonous or not. He's awfully close to you. If you move he might strike."

She quickly bent and picked up a stone, then edged toward Chris, a step at a time. "When I say go, drop as fast as you can," she murmured.

Chris tensed and watched his sister move into position. She slowly raised the stone. "Go!" she shouted.

He threw himself on the ground and heard a plop as the stone landed.

"Did you get him?" Chris yelled. He scrambled away from the bank and got to his feet.

"No," Amy said, "but I scared him. He slithered off into the woods." She made a face. "Yuck! I hate snakes! What would they be doing on this island? What do snakes eat?"

"Rats," Chris said, then wished he hadn't.

Amy gave a yelp. "I *knew* there were rats on this island!" She shuddered. "I don't think Aunt Jennie is going to want to use this place for her guests."

"Rats and snakes can be exterminated," Chris said. "They're no problem."

"What about the ghosts? Are you going to figure out a way to exterminate them, too?" For a moment Amy looked as though she was going to cry. "I want to go back to the inn."

"We will," Chris said. "But for now we have to go just a little farther."

"How much farther can we go? We must be almost at the opposite side of the island by this time."

"Not quite."

Amy looked up at the woods. "All I can see are trees. And it's steep. We're at the back of that hill."

"Want to climb it?"

"No! That snake's in there! And so are his relatives and friends!"

Chris climbed on a boulder at the other side of the little cove and looked ahead. "It's that or go back," he said. "We can't make it along the shore anymore. There's a steep, straight drop from the woods down to the water. At the bottom of the cliff are jagged rocks."

"If we go back," Amy said, "we might find Shadow there again. But if we go through the woods we don't know what we'll find."

"We'll find the house," Chris said. He tried to sound positive and reassuring.

"Are you sure you'll know the way?"

"The island isn't that big, Amy. We can't get lost. If we head into the woods here and go west, we'll come to the house."

"Which way is west?"

"Amy! Trust me."

"Shadow won't be expecting us to come from this direction, will he?" Amy asked.

"That's what I told you."

Amy managed to scramble up the bank at the edge of the woods. Clods of dirt slid from under her feet. "It's slippery," she said. "Be careful when you climb up here. That bank feels as though it's going to collapse." She picked up a small branch and flourished it in the air. "This is for hitting snakes and rats and . . . and . . . other things with," she said.

Chris fell the first time he tried to climb the bank. Finally he reached as far as he could across the top, dug in with his fingers, and finally managed to make it to the top.

"Find a stick for yourself first," Amy said.

With the number of small branches that had fallen, it took Chris only a minute to find one just the right size.

"It's getting darker," Amy said.

"Because you're in the woods."

"I'm hungry, Chris. What time do you think it is?"

"I don't know. Don't think about food. It won't help."

Chris wished that he had a wristwatch. His stomach rumbled, and he also wished he had thought of bringing something to eat.

The trees seemed to close around them, and

Chris got the uncomfortable feeling that they were being wrapped in a damp, musty blanket.

"I don't like this," Amy murmured. "Chris, something's all wrong!"

"Don't get panicky," Chris said. "Don't let your imagination get out of hand."

"Chris!" Amy's words came in short gasps. "Something's following us! It's behind us!"

Chris could feel the back of his neck begin to prickle, but he tried to remain calm. "We'll be all right as long as we stick together," he said. He stopped and turned around.

But they weren't together. Amy was running as fast as she could away from Chris and up the hill.

11

A my crashed through the underbrush, not caring about the noise she was making. Chris stumbled after her. The ground was slick with damp needles, and running was difficult.

"Amy!" he yelled. "Wait!"

One moment she was ahead of him. The next moment she had disappeared.

"Amy?"

He came to a rise and stopped. Below him the ground sloped steeply downward, ending in cliffs high above the water. To his left was a bank of rough limestone rocks.

"Amy?" he called again. "Where are you?"

Surely she hadn't fallen down that slope! He would have heard her call out, and the carpet of moss and pine needles that blanketed the slope would have been disturbed. She hadn't run back past him. But how could she have gone farther? Chris heard his own heart pounding again. What if something terrible had happened to Amy?

He edged closer to the jagged limestone bank and saw that the ground was level in front of the rocks for a width of about two feet and a distance of about twenty feet. He couldn't go down the steep slope, but on his left was the wall of limestone. Had Amy, in some mysterious way, managed to climb the rocks?

Chris edged along the level strip, facing the steep drop, his back to the rough bank. He had traveled about ten feet when suddenly someone grabbed his arm and pulled.

He was yanked off balance, staggering against the rock, which seemed to open up and swallow him.

"Hey!" he shouted.

"Be quiet, Chris! Don't make so much noise!" Amy said.

She let him go, and he saw they were standing inside a narrow opening to a cave. From what he could see, the cave was deep. The light from outside illuminated part of a high, wide room. One side was littered with dirt and clumps of grasses and pine boughs, as though it had caved in. A trickle of water ran down the other side and disappeared into the floor of the cave.

Amy frowned at him. "It's no good hiding here if you're going to make so much noise."

"If you didn't want me to make any noise, you shouldn't have grabbed me like that! What did you do that for?" Chris snapped.

"Because you were going right past the opening to the cave, that's why!"

"I was scared to death, anyway. Why did you run away?"

"I didn't run away. I just did what you told me to do."

"I told you we'd be all right as long as we stayed together."

Amy backed up against the rough rock wall and stared at Chris. "No you didn't. You told me to run to the cave as fast as I could."

"I couldn't have."

"But you did. I heard you clearly."

Chris held Amy's shoulders and looked at her carefully. "Are you trying to kid me? Because if you are, it isn't funny."

"I'm not kidding," she said. Her eyes opened wider. "Chris! Are you telling me that you weren't the one who said it?"

Chris shook his head. "How would I know there was a cave here to run to?"

"Oh. Well, because — uh — I guess you wouldn't." Amy gave a shiver and looked toward the entrance of the cave. "Then who said it?"

"What did the voice sound like?"

"I don't know. It was just — a voice."

"A man's voice?"

Amy shrugged. "No." She slid to the floor of the cave and wrapped her arms around her knees. "Chris, I just don't know."

Chris glanced around the cave. "Someone wanted us to come into the cave. I wonder why."

"It's cold in here." Amy shivered.

"Where's your sweater?"

"Back on the beach, I think."

Chris glanced at the slide at one side of the cave. "Look at that," he said. "There are some good, dry pine branches with lots of pitch in them. Why don't we light one?"

"Good idea!" Amy scrambled to her feet. "It will make us feel warmer, at least."

Chris had already picked out three of the limbs. He put one aside, took the tinder box from his pocket, and squatted next to the branch. He worked until sparks flew out and one end of the branch flared up.

He stood, picking up the branch carefully, holding it aloft. The roof, with its jagged stalactites, glittered in the light. The floor was uneven, pockmarked with small holes. Here and there a stalagmite grew under a steady drip from the roof of the cave. As he moved with the light, the wall seemed to move, too, leaping into brightness or shadow.

"Amy," Chris said, "the cave goes way back here."

"Don't leave me," Amy said.

"I'm not. Don't you want to explore a little, as long as we're here?"

Back in the shadows Chris saw something shine, then wriggle away in the darkness. Another snake? Chris didn't want to know, and he hoped Amy hadn't seen it.

"Not yet," Amy said. "For one thing, we don't know why we're supposed to be here. And for another, I think it's time to read some of Amelia's journal."

Chris walked back to where Amy was seated on a rock near the entrance, the journal unwrapped and open on her lap.

"Another voice telling you what to do?" he asked.

She shook her head. "No. Just something I want to do."

"We can't stay here, Amy."

"I know. But I have the feeling there's an answer for us in this journal. I only want a few minutes to look. Okay?"

"Well," Chris agreed grudgingly, "I'd rather look for answers in the cave."

"Ten minutes," Amy said. "That's all I want."

"You know I haven't got a watch."

"Then I'll tell you when ten minutes is up."

"You haven't got a watch, either."

"But I'll know," Amy said. "Now, hold the light over this way a little, so I can read."

Chris held the limb close to Amy, but not close enough so that a drop of pitch might hurt her. Now and then a bubble of the pitch sizzled as the wood burned, and occasionally a spark flew from the branch. Chris was glad he knew so much about surviving in the wilderness. He never thought his knowledge would come in so useful. "Are you starting at the beginning?" he asked.

"No," she said. "At the part where Amelia came to Missouri to marry Joshua Hanover." She paused. "Amelia didn't spell very well, and her handwriting is kind of spidery with curls on the letters. It's hard to read."

"Then why don't you give it up and come with me to see what's in the rest of the cave?"

Amy held up a hand to hush him. "Listen to this, Chris. She's writing here about the property. 'The pasture is wide and thick with grasses, which makes good grazing for the horse. The river beyond the house and woods is a valuable source of fish, and the woods provide fuel for the stove and fireplace. All is plentiful and good.

" 'I have discovered a quiet place, unknown to Joshua and Shadow. It is here I sometimes come when I have a few free minutes during the afternoon, when work is not too pressing. It is here I come when I want to think my own thoughts and to write them in this little book. It is my cave. My very own place. I am secure here.' "

Amy rested the book on her lap. "This cave must be the one Amelia wrote about," she said.

Chris found he was eager to hear more. "What else does she say about the cave?"

Amy silently read a few paragraphs ahead and thumbed through the rest of the pages, reading a bit here and there. She closed the book. "She doesn't mention the cave again."

Chris sat next to Amy. "Amos brought us to the island. He said he would do anything to help Amelia. And someone led us to this cave." He began to get excited. "When I walked into the Hanovers' house I stumbled on the box that held this journal, and I think now it was deliberately put in my path. It was part of the whole thing."

"Why?" Amy asked.

"Hasn't it occurred to you, Amy?" Chris asked. "It's our reason for being on this island. Amos told us to put the ghosts to rest. I think we can do it by finding Amelia."

Amy's voice was barely a whisper, and she moved closer to Chris. "How can we find Amelia?"

"By looking in this cave," Chris said. "I think she's in here with us!"

12

Amy jumped up so suddenly she dropped the journal. "Don't talk like that, Chris! You're scaring me!"

Chris got to his feet. A drop of bubbling pitch landed on one finger. "Ouch!" he yelled, and popped his finger into his mouth.

"I mean it!" Amy said. "We aren't even sure that Amelia stayed on the island. Maybe Joshua was right. Maybe she did get into the boat with the bag of money. Maybe she was glad to escape. Maybe she drowned. We don't know."

The flames at the end of the pine torch wavered and almost went out, as though a breeze had blown through the cave.

"You don't believe that," Chris said as he tried to shelter the torch.

Amy sighed. "I guess not."

Chris picked up another limb and lit the end of it from the one he was holding. "Here," he said, handing it to Amy. "Hold this away from your body. If that hot pitch drops on your hand it hurts."

Amy held it out as she turned slowly in a circle, examining what they could see of the cave. "Where do we start to look for Amelia?" she asked.

"At the far end of the cave," Chris answered.

This time Amy led the way. The room they were in became gradually narrower and lower.

"It's ending in a tunnel," Amy said. "We'll have to crawl to get into it."

"How far back does it go?" Chris asked.

Amy got on her knees and held her torch out in front of her. "Dead end," she said. She got up and brushed off the knees of her jeans.

"Did it look like a landslide had closed off this room?"

"No. It's only three or four feet deep and ends in a solid rock wall."

Chris had to look, too, just to make sure that Amy was right. The wall seemed to be an original part of the cave.

"So that's that," Amy said. She sounded relieved.

Chris glanced at the pile of rock and dirt and limbs that must have cascaded into the cave long ago. "Think about the earthquake, Amy," he said. "Amelia was terrified. She ran to a place where she had always felt protected and safe — this cave that was all her own. But she wasn't protected and safe here. The earth moved so violently that part of the roof of the cave was torn apart, and rocks and dirt and trees poured in."

Amy stared at the side of the cave. "Do you think Amelia's body is under all that?"

"Yes," Chris said. "Don't you?"

"How will we find her?"

"I wish we had a couple of shovels," Chris said, "but we don't, so we'll use our hands."

"Do we really have to look for her?" Amy asked. Then she answered her own question. "I guess we do."

"You take that side. I'll take the other," Chris said. "Find a place nearby that will hold your torch."

"This might take days and days!" Amy complained.

"I don't think so," Chris said. He propped his torch into a hole in the cave floor and got on his knees. The earth in the slide was still soft and loose, so he was able to scoop away handfuls.

Amy set to work on the other side, after she had found a place to prop her torch.

Finally Chris touched something hard. He brushed the earth away from one end of it. "Amy," he whispered. "Over here! Quick!"

Amy hurried to join him, but kept her eyes on Chris. "I'm afraid to look," she said. "Did you find — ? Is it — ?"

"It's canvas," he said. "I think it's Joshua's bag of coins. Help me get it out of here."

They scooped back the dirt until most of the bag was uncovered. Then Chris tugged it from its place. The leather strap across the top was in shreds and fell apart as they pulled at the sack. But the canvas, though worn and yellowed, seemed to hold.

Chris opened the flap on the sack, and they peered inside, almost bumping heads in their eagerness to see. The silver coins were black with tarnish, but they almost filled the sack.

"Joshua Hanover's money," Amy murmured. "We found it."

Chris put a hand into the sack and scooped up some of the coins. "If we cleaned these we could read the dates," he said. "They've got to be valuable."

Amy took a small one and turned, trying to hold it up to the light. "Is this a dime?" she asked. "Did they have dimes in 1811?"

"A coin collector could tell us all about them," Chris said.

Amy dropped the coin into the sack. "This is exciting! Just think! Now this money belongs to Aunt Jennie!" She glanced at the opening to the cave where the afternoon light was still strong. "Let's hurry and take the sack down to the beach and get our bonfire ready. We don't want to be in this cave when it gets dark."

She got to her knees, but before she could stand

Chris put out a hand and stopped her. "Not so fast," he said. "There's something we have to do first. There's something else in the hole where the sack of coins had been."

Amy bent to look. She yelped and scooted back behind Chris.

There at the back of the hole was a hand without flesh. Skeleton fingers. And through those fingers was twined a narrow, twisted chain of gold.

"We found Amelia," Chris said quietly.

"Poor Amelia," Amy said. "She really was here all along, probably killed instantly in that landslide, and for all these years mean old Joshua thought she had run away with his precious hoard of coins." She stretched around Chris's shoulder to take another look at the bony fingers, then hugged her knees and shivered. "What should we do, Chris? Do we have to do any more digging?"

"No," Chris said. "We'll leave her alone for now. We'll tell the police about it as soon as we get back, and someone will come for her body and bury it the way it should be buried."

"I could bring flowers," Amy said. "I like Amelia."

Chris stood and picked up his torch. Amy, in her eagerness, stumbled to her feet. "Do you want to carry the bag of money, or should I?" she asked.

"You're forgetting something," Chris said. "Joshua."

"I could never forget Joshua. I just want to get away from him."

"But Amos told us to put the ghosts to rest. We have to do that, Amy."

Amy shook her head angrily. "This is silly, Chris! We don't know how to put ghosts to rest! Let's get out of here while we have the chance!"

Amy stooped and picked up the sack, shifting it in her arms until she could hang on to it. "This thing is heavy," she said. She took a step toward the entrance to the cave, but Chris blocked her way.

"Put it down," he said.

"What do you mean, put it down? The money is Aunt Jennie's now, isn't it?"

Chris reached for the sack, saying, "You can't take it out of here!"

Amy shouted, "Leave me alone! Stop it, Chris!" She hugged the sack, digging in with her fingernails, and tried to reach the cave entrance.

Chris dropped his torch and pulled on Amy and the sack.

Suddenly the sack seemed to disintegrate, and Amy and Chris staggered backward. The coins spilled to the floor of the cave.

"Oh, no!" Chris said.

"Look what we've done to Aunt Jennie's money!" Amy cried.

Chris stared at the coins and shook his head. He dropped the piece of sack that he was still holding. "Those coins don't belong to Aunt Jennie yet," he said. "They're still the property of Joshua Hanover."

"But he's dead."

Chris stepped over the coins to face Amy. "I know you're eager to get off this island and to take the coins to Aunt Jennie, but think about it, Amy. As long as the ghosts of Joshua Hanover and Shadow prowl around this island, it won't be of any use to Aunt Jennie. We have to give this money back to Joshua Hanover. After he realizes that his wife didn't run away with his money, that she died here on the island, and that his coins are still here, then he can be satisfied."

"You think that he'll leave the island then?"

"Yes. I do."

"But how do we tell him about Amelia and the money? We can't just walk up to a ghost and talk to him. He doesn't seem to be the kind of ghost who'd want to listen, either."

"We lure him to this cave," Chris said.

"How do we do that?"

"I've got an idea that might work."

"Tell me about it," Amy said.

But before Chris had a chance to say a word, a shadow darkened the entrance to the cave, and a low growl echoed through the room. Chris and Amy quickly turned toward the sound. There, blocking the way, stood Shadow.

13

Chris slowly bent and picked up his torch.

"He found us!" Amy whispered.

Shadow growled again, and Amy shivered.

"He won't hurt us," Chris said.

"How do you know that?"

"I don't know it," Chris said. "I'm guessing that because he's a ghost he's limited to another plane and can't physically enter our plane and harm us." He sighed. "Amy, I'm saying all this to make myself feel better."

Shadow sat in the doorway as though he was guarding it.

"I wonder how he found this cave," Amy said.

"I think he knew about it all along," Chris said. "Look at him. Did you ever see a dog in new territory? He stares and sniffs around to scout it out. Shadow acts as though he's known about this cave for a long time."

"Maybe he followed Amelia on some of her visits

here before the earthquake happened."

"I bet he did, but he stayed far enough back so that Amelia didn't know he was there."

"I wonder," Amy said, "if he's known that Amelia and the sack of Joshua's money were here all these years."

Shadow's lips pulled back in a snarl.

"He did!" she said. "I'm sure of it! But why didn't he want Joshua to know?"

"Because he was jealous of Amelia," Chris said. "Amos told us so. He said that Shadow didn't like her."

"That dog is horrible. He'd rather see his master rage around the island for years and years than help him find out the truth."

Shadow rose and took a step inside the cave.

Chris handed his torch to Amy. "Keep this between Shadow and us. He doesn't like the fire."

"What are you going to do?"

"Get what we'll need to lure Joshua to the cave."

"What's that?"

But Chris didn't answer. As quickly as he could he dropped to his knees and reached back into the hole they had made in the earth slide. His fingers met Amelia's dry bones. For an instant he shuddered and pulled back, but he made himself reach out again and pull the twisted gold chain from the skeleton's hand.

When he stood up he held it out to Amy to see. Shadow's eyes narrowed. He snarled and backed into the entrance of the cave.

"This is what we'll need," he said. "Joshua will recognize it." He put the gold chain in his pocket.

"Shadow recognizes it, too," Amy whispered. "Look at him. I think he's scared. Is it possible to frighten a ghost? That sounds backward, doesn't it? Yes, it does, because normally ghosts frighten people."

"Stop talking to yourself and follow me," Chris said. He picked up Amy's torch and began walking toward Shadow.

Shadow didn't move. His lips curled to expose his teeth, and his fangs gleamed.

"Get out of here, Shadow," Chris said, "or we'll walk right through you!"

"Can we do that?" Amy whispered.

"Watch us!" Chris said.

But as Chris approached, his torch held out, Shadow backed away and disappeared.

"How will we know where he is?" Amy asked.

"We won't," Chris said. "We'll just have to be cautious."

"I think he's going to try to stop us from seeing Joshua."

"How?"

"We'll find out."

Chris didn't expect to find out quite so soon. He

and Amy left the cave and stood on the level ledge outside, blinking, trying to accustom their eyes to the daylight. "The sky isn't as overcast as it was this morning," Chris said. "I don't think it's going to rain after all." He studied the sky. "I guess that it's around four or five o'clock. What do you think?"

But Amy didn't look at the sky. She was staring down the slick slope to the edge of the cliff.

"When I ran to the cave I guess I didn't even notice that slope," Amy said. "It's almost like a slide. What's at the bottom of those cliffs?"

"Big, jagged rocks," Chris said. "Walk carefully. The ledge we're on isn't very wide."

Amy turned and walked just a few steps when suddenly Shadow, barking and snarling, rushed right at her. Amy shrieked and jumped back, slamming into Chris and knocking him to one side. Chris reached out, but there was nothing to hold on to. With a yell he fell face down onto the slick pine needles and damp grasses and slid like a rocket toward the edge of the cliff. His torch bounced and rolled ahead of him. He heard a splash as it fell.

He dug in the toes of his shoes, trying to break his speed, but he was moving too fast. It slowed his speed a little, but not enough. Chris skidded to the edge of the cliff and went over.

He heard Amy screaming, and he wanted to

scream, too, but it was all he could do to cling to some clumps of grass near the edge of the cliff. The earth was moist, and he knew the grass wouldn't hold for long. Luckily, he found footholds in the rough rock. A tangle of roots protruded from near the top of the bank, and he used it to pull against as he hoisted himself up and over the edge. Digging away layers of the needles, he carved himself a nest and lay there, breathing heavily and resting.

"Chris!" Amy yelled. "I'll come and get you!"

Chris raised his head. "No! Stay there! Better yet, make your way back to level land under the pines. Find a safe spot to stand in, and don't let anything scare you into moving from that spot!"

After he had rested for a few moments, Chris began working his way up the slope, brushing the damp pine needles out of his way, making sure he had solid handholds of grass to hang on to. It seemed to be slow going, but soon Chris had reached the ledge. He sat up and looked around for Amy.

She was standing in the woods, just where he had told her to stand. She had stuck the unlit end of the torch into the ground near her feet. Tears were on her face, and she cried out, "Oh, Chris! I thought I'd killed you!"

Chris slowly climbed to his feet and made his way toward her. When he got to his sister he hugged her. "It wasn't your fault, Amy. It was

Shadow's. We'll have to be very, very careful."

"I feel as though he's watching us." Amy stepped back and looked to each side.

"We won't let him stop us," Chris said. "We'll find Joshua Hanover."

"Where will we look?"

"At the top of the pasture, near the edge of the woods."

Amy gulped. "You mean at Shadow's grave! Oh, Chris! Let's not go there!"

"Can you think of a better place to look?"

"How about back at Joshua's house? You wanted to go there again."

"Just to look for some kind of clue about what we were supposed to do. Now we know."

"Maybe Joshua went to the beach. We could look there."

"You're stalling, Amy," Chris said. "Let's go." He began walking through the woods in what he hoped was the right direction. Amy stayed close by his side. Chris wished there had been some kind of path, and he looked for signs that Amelia might have made to mark the way, but there were none. The overgrown pine woods were dark and still. In places there was a great deal of underbrush, and sometimes they had to climb over a fallen pine tree. Chris moved cautiously, because he wanted to be aware of anything that Shadow might try.

As Chris and Amy walked they occasionally heard a low growling. Sometimes it was behind them, sometimes in front, sometimes at one side or the other, but at no time did Shadow appear.

"Look," Amy said. "It's getting lighter! We must be near the edge of the forest."

She and Chris began to run and soon broke through the trees. They found themselves standing at the edge of the pasture.

"We're almost at the top of the hill!" Chris said.

"Then we must be near Shadow's grave."

Amy and Chris glanced to their right and gasped. There — just a few feet away from them — stood both Shadow and Joshua Hanover.

Joshua raised both fists, and his face was thunderous with rage. "Vengeance!" he shouted in a voice that was raspy and hollow.

Chris felt his knees wobble as though all the bones in his legs had fallen out, but he managed to take a step toward the ghost. "Mr. Hanover," he said. "We found — "

But his words were drowned out by Shadow's furious barking.

Joshua glared at Chris. "Go! Get off my property!"

"But — "

"Show him the gold chain," Amy said.

Shadow suddenly dashed forward, whining and barking, and raced down the hill toward the house.

Joshua called, "Shadow! Here, Shadow!" and strode down the hill after him.

Chris tugged the chain from his pocket and held it out in shaking fingers as Joshua passed them. "Look at this!" he shouted.

Joshua's glance swept across Chris and Amy, but he didn't seem to notice the gold chain. In an instant he had disappeared.

Chris stuffed the chain back into his pocket. He had never felt so discouraged. "I thought it would work."

Amy leaned against the nearest tree trunk. "Shadow's going back to the house," she said.

"What are we going to do about him?" Chris asked. "He's going to try anything he can to keep Joshua from finding Amelia and the money."

"Then we'll try harder," Amy said. "If Joshua won't *listen* to you, then maybe we can do something to make him *see* what we have."

"Like what? He didn't even look at the gold chain."

"Maybe we need something bigger. I have sort of an idea," Amy said, "but we'll have to go inside the house to find out if it will work."

"What's your idea?"

"Clothes," Amy said. "Maybe whatever clothes Amelia and Joshua wore have fallen to rags by this time. But if they haven't, and we dressed in them, it might get Joshua's attention, and you could show him Amelia's gold chain."

"I guess it's worth a try," Chris answered. "Let's follow them to the house."

They ran down the hill, but there was no sign of Joshua or Shadow outside the house. The front door still hung open. Chris stuck his head inside and listened. There wasn't a sound.

"If Shadow and Joshua are inside I don't know how I'll get the courage to go in there, too," Amy said.

"I don't think they're in the house," Chris said. "It's as silent as a — uh — grave."

They stepped over the sill and entered the house. Amy looked around the main room. "Where's the bedroom?"

"There are some doors off the kitchen," Chris said. "From the shape of the house I'd guess there's a bedroom at the opposite side of the door to the cellar."

They walked through the kitchen, their footsteps loud in the silence. Just as Chris had thought, there was a door at the far side. He was prepared to work hard to open it, as he had the door to the cellar, but this swung open easily as he turned the knob.

The room was small. On one side was a small, high window. Its lower edge glittered with a few shards of broken glass. Under the window were a chest and a small chair. The chair was on its side and a lamp lay shattered next to it. A bed was wedged against the north wall. The cotton blanket on the bed was covered with mold, and dust lay like an extra blanket over it and the chest.

"Where is the closet?" Amy asked, as she turned in a full circle.

"People didn't build closets into their houses then," Chris said. "They didn't have many clothes, so they kept the ones they weren't wearing in chests. Sometimes they hung them in a wardrobe, but there aren't any wardrobes in here, so the clothes must be in the chest."

"How come you know all these things?" Amy asked.

"I told you. In my school project about the pioneers — "

"Okay!" Amy said, clapping her hands over her ears. "I believe you!"

She jerked up the heavy lid of the chest and propped it against the wall. Inside the chest were some cloths and towels and exactly what Amy was looking for — some neatly folded clothing.

She held up a brown cotton dress. "It's kind of fragile, but I think it will hold together." She slipped it over her head and turned her back to Chris. "Will you button it up for me?"

"It fits you," Chris said. "Amelia must have been awfully short and skinny."

"Thanks a lot," Amy said. She twirled around. "I wish I had a mirror."

Chris pulled some things from the chest, examined them, and shook his head. "There's nothing in here that would fit me," he said.

"It doesn't matter," Amy said. "This dress might be enough to get Joshua's attention."

"We'll go outside," Chris said. "Maybe it will help if we call him."

Together they moved toward the door, but it suddenly slammed in their faces with a crash.

Chris pulled and tugged at the knob, but the door didn't budge.

"Amy," he said. "We're locked in!"

14

Amy was already climbing on top of the chest. "Then we'll go out this way," she said. She gingerly picked the slivers of glass from the window frame, dropping them on the floor. "Give me a boost," she said.

Chris climbed on the chest, too, keeping his weight on the frame of the chest, hoping the top wouldn't cave in. He boosted Amy up to the window. "Can you make it?" he asked.

"Sure," she said. She squiggled around so that she could go through the window feet first. "It's not much of a drop to the ground."

Her fingers let go of their hold on the frame, and he heard her land with a thud on the other side.

"Are you okay?" he called.

"Yes. Hurry!" she said.

Chris easily hoisted himself up and through the small window, jumping down to the ground.

"Hurry!" Amy whispered.

"What's the rush?"

"Haven't you noticed?" she said. "The light's getting dimmer. I think pretty soon it will be dark."

Chris studied the sky. "We've got about an hour," he said.

"Or less," Amy said. "Hurry! I'm getting even more scared! We can't stay on this island after dark!"

Chris stepped away from the house. "Where to?" he asked. "Back to the graves?"

Amy shuddered. "I guess so. I don't know where else to try to find Joshua. Do you?"

Chris took Amy's hand and pulled her with him out into the pasture. "Let's try something else. Let's call him! I bet sometimes Amelia did that, when she wanted him to come for dinner or needed him for something."

They yelled together at the top of their lungs, "Joshua Hanover!"

Then they listened. Not a sound could be heard on the island. Amy's fingers tightened in Chris's hand. "It's getting dark fast," she said.

"Faster than I thought it would," Chris said. "But we've still got about half an hour."

"And then what happens?" Amy asked. "Don't ghosts have more power at night?"

"I honestly don't know," Chris said. "I never believed in ghosts until we came to this island."

"Let's yell again," Amy said.

"You yell, and I'll be quiet," Chris said. "Maybe he'll think you're Amelia."

Amy did, calling Joshua's name over and over again.

Chris grabbed her shoulder. "There he is!" he whispered.

From up on the hill strode the long, scarecrow figure of Joshua Hanover, Shadow beside him. Even in the dim light of evening they could see the tormented expression on his face.

"I don't think he likes it that I'm wearing Amelia's clothes," Amy said.

"But we did get his attention," Chris said. He pulled out the gold chain.

Shadow ran toward Chris, snapping and barking.

"You're not going to win this time," Chris yelled at Shadow. He took a few steps toward Shadow, who didn't have time to back up, and walked right through him. Shadow vanished.

Joshua stopped in front of them. Chris held out the gold chain to him.

But Joshua didn't react as Chris thought he would. He stopped and gave a loud, agonizing cry. Again, he raised his fists high in the air, squeezed his eyes shut, and wailed, "Amelia!"

Amy, tears on her cheeks, cried out, "I'm not Amelia, Mr. Hanover! I'm Amy Holt, and I didn't mean to hurt you!"

"Come with us. Please!" Chris said to Joshua.

Joshua opened his eyes. "Betrayed," he whispered to Amy. Then he turned toward Chris. He growled almost as Shadow had growled and came toward Chris with his hands outstretched, as though he was going to grab him and not the chain.

"Run!" Amy yelled at Chris. "Run toward the cave!"

The forest was so dark now it was hard to make their way through it, but Chris and Amy scrambled as fast as they could go. A few times Chris turned and saw that Joshua was following them. An evil smirk had replaced the anger. What did he plan to do to them?

They reached the edge of the slope and the path to the cave. The smoldering torch was a bright spot that marked their way. "Now what?" Amy asked. She leaned against a tree, panting for breath.

"Get behind the tree," Chris said. "I'm going to lure Joshua into the cave."

"He doesn't understand what we're doing," Amy said. "I don't think he knows that the chain belongs to Amelia."

"But when he sees the journal and the money, he'll know," Chris said.

"Did you see his face? We didn't mean to hurt him, but we did, and now he wants to hurt us."

"We haven't got a choice," Chris said. "It's the only thing left to do. Hurry up. Hide!"

Chris turned to see that Joshua was standing only a few feet from them. "Joshua," he said. "Come with me." Again he held out the gold chain.

For the first time Joshua seemed to see the chain. He looked puzzled. He took a step toward Chris.

"Look out," Amy whispered. "Shadow's guarding the cave!"

Chris picked up the torch. He slowly backed onto the level strip in front of the limestone bank. He edged his way toward the entrance of the cave. Joshua slowly followed him.

As he came close to the entrance Shadow suddenly leaped toward him. Chris flattened himself against the wall. "You won't get me this time," he yelled at Shadow.

Chris heard a growl over his head. He looked up to see Shadow at the top of the limestone bank. With teeth bared, Shadow jumped right at Chris.

This time Chris held the torch high, aiming it at Shadow. As the torch passed through the ghost dog, Shadow yelped and vanished.

Just two steps further and Chris was at the entrance of the cave. "Come," he said to Joshua. "Come and see."

He entered the cave and stuck the unlit end of the torch into a crack in the cave floor. It gave enough light so that the scattered coins could be seen. Chris hurried to place the gold chain just inside the large hole they had dug. If Joshua saw it he would be able to see the bones of Amelia's hand.

Chris stood against the wall of the cave and wished he was invisible. He waited.

Where was Joshua?

Just when Chris was about to give up, the entrance to the cave became dark. From where he was pressed against the wall Chris could see Joshua peering into the cave.

A horrible cry echoed through the cave. Joshua's ghost stumbled to its knees, and tried to scoop up handfuls of the coins. He moaned and muttered to himself, as Chris slowly edged closer and closer to the opening in the cave.

Then Shadow slunk into the cave like an evil shadow. Silently he slipped around Joshua and sat in front of the hole that Chris had dug, his tongue hanging out, a wicked look in his eyes.

"Oh no you don't!" Chris yelled at Shadow. He picked up a small stone and hurled it at the dog.

Shadow, true to form, left his spot to snarl and threaten Chris.

Chris didn't care. Shadow couldn't hurt him. Joshua had seen the gold chain, and beyond the chain to the bony hand. Joshua's wail bounced off the walls of the cave.

There was nothing more Chris could do. He

hurried out of the cave and made his way along the track as fast as he could without stumbling. Amy was waiting for him and grabbed his arms, pulling him into the woods.

"What happened?" she asked.

Suddenly the cave seemed to explode with a gigantic roar. Chris and Amy were knocked off their feet by a swift rush of wind.

It was over almost as soon as it had begun. Amy raised her head. "What was that?"

Chris sat up. "Listen," he said.

The forest had come alive with sound. There was a soft soughing in the pine trees, and a bird chirped somewhere over their heads. They could hear the splash of wavelets against the rocks and the motor from a boat far out on the river.

"Shall we go back to the cave?" Amy asked.

"Not now," Chris said. "It's going to be dark soon."

He and Amy got to their feet. There was just enough daylight left for them to trace their steps back to the beach.

"Look at our pile of wood!" Amy said. "What happened?"

The pile was stacked high, as they had originally left it.

"Maybe when we thought it was scattered along the beach it really wasn't," Amy continued. "I mean, it might have been an illusion, and we thought — Well, it could have been that way. Or could it?"

"Stop talking to yourself and hold this," Chris said, handing her a short stick of the pine. He pulled the tinder box from his pocket and set to work with the flint and steel. In just a moment the pine had caught. He thrust the flaming branch into the pile of logs and boughs, and the whole thing caught with a whoosh.

Chris and Amy stepped back from the blaze.

"Mom and Aunt Jennie will see the fire," Amy said.

"They'll send a boat," Chris said. "I don't think we'll have long to wait."

Amy sat on the beach, pulling her knees up and hugging her legs. She rested her chin on her knees. "I'm not afraid anymore," she said. "I like the island now. It's just the way it should be."

"We'll have a lot to tell everyone," Chris said.

"They won't believe us." Amy sighed.

"But when they go to the cave they'll be able to see the coins and the gold chain and — and Amelia," Chris said.

"I mean they won't believe about the ghosts and what they did. You can't see ghosts."

"But if we explain."

"You didn't believe in ghosts until you actually saw one," Amy said. "Mom and Aunt Jennie and everyone else will just think we came over here, and our boat sunk, and we went exploring and found the cave and Amelia's body. If we tell them about the ghosts they'll just say that we have 'lively imaginations.' "

Chris sat down next to her. "I suppose you're right. Don't you think anyone will believe our story?"

Amy shrugged. "Maybe someday we'll write it down, and someone will read it and believe it."

"Maybe," Chris said. He could see the lights along the opposite shore. A few of them seemed to be moving closer. He thought he heard the motor of a boat.

"There's just one thing I wish," Amy said. She looked toward the bonfire. "I wish I had a marshmallow."

A voice called from a short distance away on the water, "Amy! Chris! Are you there?"

The boat was coming closer.

About the Author

JOAN LOWERY NIXON is the award-winning author of more than fifty books for young people (among them *The House on Hackman's Hill*), two thirds of them mysteries. The inspiration for her books frequently comes from news stories or true incidents, to which she adds her own special twists. She is a two-time winner of the Edgar Allan Poe award, and she lives with her family in Texas.